DEATH ON THE DOWN BEAT

DEATH ON THE DOWN BEAT

AN ORCHESTRAL FANTASY OF DETECTION

SEBASTIAN FARR

With an Introduction by
Martin Edwards

Poisoned Pen
PRESS

Introduction © 2022, 2023 by Martin Edwards
Death on the Down Beat © 1941 by The Estate of Eric Walter Blom
Cover and internal design © 2023 by Sourcebooks
Front cover image © Mary Evans Picture Library

Published by Poisoned Pen Press, an imprint of Sourcebooks,
in association with the British Library
P.O. Box 4410, Naperville, Illinois 60567-4410
(630) 961-3900
sourcebooks.com

Death on the Down Beat was first published in the UK
in 1941 by J. M. Dent & Sons, Ltd, London.

Cataloging-in-Publication Data is on file with the Library of Congress.

Printed and bound in the United States of America.
KP 10 9 8 7 6 5 4 3 2 1

Introduction

Death on the Down Beat, originally published in 1941, is subtitled "An Orchestral Fantasy of Detection." This is a highly unusual detective novel which is likely to appeal particularly to music lovers. A rare and little-known novel, it has nevertheless been described by the Golden Age mystery aficionado Barry Pike in *The Oxford Companion to Crime & Mystery Writing* as an "epistolary tour de force."

Music quite often accompanies the action in detective stories (one example among many is Cyril Hare's enjoyable novel *When the Wind Blows*), but here it reaches a crescendo of significance. Sir Noel Grampian, the unpopular conductor of the Maningpool Municipal Orchestra, is sensationally shot dead during a performance of Strauss's tone poem "A Hero's Life." In many vintage mysteries, readers are provided with a map of the location or the floor plan of a country house which was the scene of the crime. Here, the supplementary material includes a diagram showing the layout of the orchestra, a page from the symphony concert programme, and no fewer than four pages of musical notation— all of which contain information relevant to the plot.

The story is told mainly through letters sent by Detective Inspector Alan Hope of New Scotland Yard to his wife, Julia. These are supplemented by information from newspaper cuttings and an extensive selection of letters from members of the orchestra who might be able to cast light on the killing. The late

Sir Noel had the unfortunate habit of making enemies which characterises so many murder victims in detective fiction, but there are surprisingly few physical clues to the crime. As Alan complains, "At the outset there were over 2,000 suspects... However, the audience is definitely eliminated... The orchestra alone... is really under suspicion, and quite enough, too." The pool of suspects is reduced further, so as to comprise the "permanent members" of the orchestra, but among them, motives to dispose of Sir Noel abound. A correspondent for a local newspaper advances the argument that "without a study of the score of Strauss's ["A Hero's Life"], no solution of the mystery can be profitably attempted." Eventually, snippets of information gleaned from the documentary material put Alan on the right track.

The unorthodoxy of the story is fascinating, and there is some truth in the claim on the dust jacket of the first edition: "Here is something new in detective fiction." That said, this book is also an intriguing example of the "casebook" type of crime fiction whose ancestry can be traced back to the nineteenth century. Notable early examples include Wilkie Collins's *The Moonstone*, while Golden Age variations include *S. S. Murder* by Q. Patrick and *The Documents in the Case* by Dorothy L. Sayers and Robert Eustace. This is a form of storytelling which is inherently flexible, and successful modern variations on the theme include Iain Pears's *An Instance of the Fingerpost* and Lucy Foley's *The Hunting Party*.

Edmund Crispin, a leading Golden Age detective novelist who achieved distinction as a composer under his real name, Bruce Montgomery, regarded *Death on the Down Beat* as a masterpiece. Nicholas Blake, in a review for the *Spectator*, said:

"Musicians will appreciate both the deductions made from the musical score and the milieu of a provincial orchestra—to say nothing of the amusing feud between Maningpool's two music critics."

Sebastian Farr's publishers, J. M. Dent, made a mystery of his identity. This was a marketing gimmick that Victor Gollancz had employed memorably with the first two books published by Anthony Berkeley Cox under the name Francis Iles. *"Who is Sebastian Farr?"* was the question emblazoned on the rear cover of the dust wrapper. According to the blurb on the first edition: "'Sebastian Farr' is the pen-name of a well-known musician, who is likely to find new fame as a conductor of criminal investigation. His plot is ingenious. He is, moreover, a writer of uncommon gifts. This is (forgive the pun) a farr, farr better thing than the average detective story."

Whether or not one is prepared to forgive the pun, those were bold words. Unfortunately, the book, like so many novels written during wartime, disappeared almost without trace. It may be as a result of disappointment that Sebastian Farr never returned for an encore. However, he achieved considerable success as a journalist and editor. In real life, he was Eric Walter Blom (1888–1959), who was born in German-speaking Switzerland and was of partly Danish descent. He moved to Britain and spent his working life there.

While working for a music publisher, Blom taught himself music and started writing programme notes for Henry Wood's concerts. His first post as a music critic was with the *Manchester Guardian*, as it was then known; he wrote notices of events in London from 1923–31. He was with the *Birmingham Post* for the next fifteen years before moving to London, mainly in order to work on the fifth edition of *Grove's Dictionary of Music and Musicians*, a monumental work in nine volumes. He became chief music critic for the *Observer*, and his last article for that newspaper, on Handel, appeared the day after his death. He had a particular enthusiasm for Mozart.

According to his obituary in *The Times* (which made no mention of this novel), he was "shy but not unsociable and he had an almost feline wit. He was public-spirited in his voluntary work...which included the chairmanship of the Central Music Library and membership of several advisory panels. For these distinguished services to music he was made C.B.E. in 1955 and awarded a D. Litt by Birmingham University in the same year." He married in 1923, and they had a son and a daughter, Celia, who married the journalist Paul Jennings and illustrated some of his books.

Martin Edwards
www.martinedwardsbooks.com

A Note from the Publisher

Thursday, 29th September 1938

ERRINGTON WELLS, 9.55 P.M.—HOPE, LARCHWOOD, CARTERFIELD—NOT HOME TOMORROW— CALAMITY AT MANINGPOOL CONCERT—GRAMPIAN DEAD—SEE MORNING PAPERS—ASKING YARD LET ME TAKE CHARGE—WRITING—LOVE—ALAN.

VALEVIEW HOTEL,
ERRINGTON WELLS.
Thursday Night.

DEAREST JULIA,

This is just to confirm my wire and to explain, in great haste. I am off back to Maningpool early in the morning. Humphrey Gillighan telephoned in a fearful state about 9.30, asking me to come back. It would have saved a lot of trouble if I'd stayed on with them another day or two. You will have seen the papers by the time you get this, so I won't go into details. (Plenty of details to come later, you poor dear.) Grampian was shot dead in the middle of the concert last night, the very concert, if you please, which I came here to avoid, barbarian that I am. Beatrice was to play in the orchestra, and I couldn't have refused to go. It appears that she always plays second harp parts at their symphony concerts whenever they are wanted, not to oblige her precious brother-in-law (I may speak ill of the dead to *you*, if they are dead of *that* sort), but simply as a hobby. She loves it, and I think it's rather nice of her not to be stuck-up about it, just because she is the wife of the Prof. of Music and the Chairman of the Orchestra Committee (same person, she not being a bigamist!). The Committee, they told me, loves it even more: it saves them a fee.

But I mustn't be flippant. It's going to be desperately serious. I've no doubt that old Higgy will let me take charge, as I asked him by wire at once. I shall hear in the course of the morning, I daresay. I only wish now I *had* gone to the beastly concert, but the prospect bored me dreadfully. And I couldn't confess it to anyone but you, though you *are* a veritable St. Cecilia. Well, you just understand—not only music, but unmusical me. Two up for you, my sweet. But what a husband for you!

Oh, yes, I shan't be back at the G.s', of course. Heaven forbid. Imagine the fuss in that house. What I shall want is peace and time to think. The Four Georges for me: it's a good pub, and no nonsense.

That's all, except love to you and the kids. Sorry not to see you. Oh, and of course I'll send you the usual confidential dossier. No doubt you'll help me in solving the mystery—if mystery there's going to be—especially this time, as it's to do with music and I'm such an outsider. Anyhow, you're always a grand help, if you do nothing more than receive my outpourings, which will begin to-morrow, I expect. They clarify my fuddled mind—so bear with me once again. And please keep everything, in the order in which I send it—my letters and anything that may accompany them. I needn't ask you to put it all in the safe the moment you've done with it. Yet isn't that a way of asking? I'm a fusspot. However, I fuss politely, at least.

Of course the old qualms will arise once again, as we both

have remnants of a conscience left. Should an officer of Scotland Yard confide in his wife, to the extent even of placing documents, or copies of documents, in her hands, before a case is finished and done with and published? Well, it always comes to this, as far as I am concerned: your letting me down in any way is such an inconceivably horrible tragedy that I cannot imagine my wanting to keep my job if that happened. But one must put one's complete trust in *someone*, particularly if one is professionally so constantly reminded of the appalling variety of frailty and unreliability in human nature. One would go mad otherwise in a life like mine.

Take care of yourselves, all of you,

Ever thine own,

ALAN.

PAPERS
PRIVATE AND CONFIDENTIAL

SENT TO

JULIA HOPE

BY HER HUSBAND

DETECTIVE-INSPECTOR ALAN HOPE
OF
NEW SCOTLAND YARD

Friday, 30th September

FOUR GEORGES HOTEL,
MANINGPOOL.

30. IX. 38.

DARLING,

A frantic day. Local police very decent, giving me full details
of last night. Their doctor, too: good chap, though a little long-
suffering at first, having to repeat it all to me. There's no doubt, I
ought to have been at that concert.

There's been no time to think. That will come to-night, no
doubt. Not that it'll keep me awake. You know how I've learnt,
from sheer necessity, to shut it all out, like a publican at closing-
time, and make myself go off to sleep as though I'd put a toy
away in the cupboard. But no use going into details now. I will
to-morrow. It will do me good, and it does always clear my mind,
if you can bear with me once again. Not that you *need* read it, you
know that; only you always do, bless you.

I'll type my letters to save you eye-strain and myself writer's
cramp, with carbon copies. Press cuttings like the enclosed I'll get
in duplicate. Anything else I'll ask the locals to copy. They have
admirable typists with nothing to do, so they are kind enough
to tell me. Here's the Press dope about the affair, to start with.
It suggests some things. I'm asking the Yard on the strength of
it to send Ailner down to Harmsford to ferret out that unpleas-
antness of Grampian's. It sounds promising, and if it does not
link up with anything here, it will tell me something about the
chap, though you can imagine the Gillighans know a good deal.

Beatrice's manner, I noticed, invariably became subacid when her dear brother-in-law was mentioned, and why her sister Letty has never lived here I can't yet fathom. The obituary, you see, is non-committal on the point.

I'm sending only the stuff from the *M'pool Telegraph*, one of the few decent provincial papers left. The rival one, the *Messenger*, is no good. That *may* be amusing, in which case I'll cut it to ribbons for you. But here's enough to go on with.

The hotel really is quite jolly. I don't know whether it was founded in the reign of one of its four patron sinners, but it does have something of the old coaching inn about it still, including a French-looking *porte cochère* with a yard behind it which only needs galleries to look the real thing. And, bless it, it has a coffee room and a smoke (no, not smoking) room. I don't know why. People can smoke wherever they like and they don't want to drink the hotel coffee anywhere. At least I don't. Otherwise the cooking is excellent, probably the more so because they have not yet taken to calling it cuisine. It's plain, rather, though we did have guinea-fowl to-night with the proper trimmings, and I don't care a rap whether it's wholesome; I simply find it good. And you know I don't suspect cooking merely because it is elaborate any more than I would suspect your virtue because you use lipstick. But enough, as I said five or six pages back.

Ever in plighted troth,

Yours,

ALAN.

Love to the kids. When *shall* I see them?

Three cuttings from *The Maningpool Telegraph*

TRAGIC DEATH OF SIR NOEL GRAMPIAN

SHOT DURING PERFORMANCE
Symphony Concert Calamity

We regret to announce the sudden and violent death of Sir Noel Grampian, the eminent conductor of the Maningpool Municipal Orchestra, at the Civic Hall during the Symphony Concert last night. There is, unfortunately, no doubt whatever that the popular conductor was shot, and as shooting at a concert cannot possibly be an accidental affair, the only conclusion to be arrived at, much as one may hesitate to put the matter into cold print at so early a stage, is that Sir Noel was murdered.

Unfortunately the Police have no clue at the moment as to who may have committed so foul a deed, but as Sir Noel was undoubtedly shot from the front while he was in the act of conducting, it is thought to be quite conclusively proved, incredible though it may seem, that the crime is to be laid at the door of a member of the orchestra. No doubt this seems inconceivable where people engaged in the gentle Art of Music are concerned, but we must resign ourselves to facts. However, we trust at least that members of the permanent orchestra may be exonerated, for, as it happened, a large number of extra players engaged from here, there and everywhere were performing with the Municipal Orchestra when this sad calamity occurred, and it is not beyond imagination that some undesirable element may have thus intruded into the rank and file.

The Police officers on duty at the concert, according to the usual routine, succeeded in having all the doors of the Civil Hall closed, it is thought, before any one could escape. At any rate, the whole orchestra was present at the preliminary investigation instituted as soon as higher Police officials had been summoned, and while every player was closely questioned and names and addresses were verified, the general public was allowed to go home, there being no possibility that the shot could have come from the auditorium. It would in any case have been impossible to retain and examine nearly 2,000 people, and it will be quite difficult enough, we imagine, to make the necessary investigations among the members of the orchestra, permanent and temporary. It is thought, however, *The Maningpool Telegraph* learns from an authoritative source, that an examination will reveal the direction in which the shot was fired, and that this will lead to the elimination of a large number of people who could not, from their positions on the platform, have committed the crime.

It is not yet known whether any detentions have been effected, nor whether the Maningpool Police will deal with the case or call in Scotland Yard.

An account of the tragedy by an eye-witness, and an obituary notice of Sir Noel Grampian, will be found elsewhere in this issue.

SIR NOEL GRAMPIAN SHOT

UPHEAVAL AT THE CIVIC HALL
(From an Eye-Witness)

I was sitting peacefully in the front row of the upper gallery at the Civic Hall, drinking in eagerly the gorgeous sounds of Richard Strauss in "A Hero's Life," and little dreaming of grim realities. Suddenly, just after a glorious climax, I noticed Sir Noel Grampian, never a quiet figure in front of an orchestra, giving a frantic wave with his baton that seemed to have nothing to do with the music. Not knowing the work well, having only played it once as a piano duet with a friend from a copy borrowed from our splendid Public Library, I could not make out what was happening, or whether such extraordinary gesticulating was really required there, nor did I remember exactly what was going to happen in the music. But there was a curious kind of sagging going on which did not seem to make a natural descent from the climax.

It was a matter of only a second or two, and it took much less time to think these conflicting thoughts than to reveal them on paper. Then, the music still going on in a broken sort of way, Sir Noel suddenly swayed backwards, as if he were going to fall over the bars of his rostrum and crash on to the floor below, in front of the well-dressed ladies and gentlemen in the stalls. He seemed to grip his waistcoat violently with his left hand (near his heart, I suppose), still brandishing his stick jerkily with his right, and then he lurched forward, caught himself for a second or two on his desk, which fell over and cast off the full score, whereupon he pitched head foremost down in front of the rostrum, into a kind of well before the nearest players. It looked as though there should have been an appalling thud, as he did not hold out his hands in front of him to save himself, I think, but crashed straight on his head. But nothing was heard, as the music was still proceeding in that broken, desultory way. Only then did every instrument come to a dead stop, and I saw two or three of the string players get up and come to Sir Noel's assistance. But he was by then quite motionless and appeared to be dead.

The remarkable thing is that I heard no shot, and none of the people I asked afterwards had any idea of how the accident, as they supposed it to be, had happened, for they too had heard nothing. Everybody thought, I suppose, as I did, that it was a case of heart-failure or some such seizure. It was not until one of the police officers who had caused the doors to be closed spoke of shooting and warned the audience that they might be detained, as indeed we were for a time, that anybody realised that a shot had been fired, and indeed a murder committed. It may seem surprising that no report was noticed, but it must be remembered that Strauss's music makes a good deal of noise which could easily cover up a shot, and even if it did not do so, if an experiment were made and a report actually expected, the case would be very different where nobody could have thought of such a thing and every listener was strung up to a high pitch of excitement by the thrilling music of "A Hero's Life" and, I may say, Sir Noel's wonderful conducting.

But that excitement was as nothing to what we all went through at this concert afterwards. I, for one, shall never forget the terrible impression made on me by the dreadful death of one who, in my humble opinion, was one of the greatest conductors who ever existed.

OBITUARIES

SIR NOEL GRAMPIAN

Sir Noel Grampian, accounts of whose tragic death last night will be found on another page, was one of the most remarkable musical personalities of the present day, in this country, or indeed anywhere. Maningpool was none the less honoured by his engagement as conductor of the Municipal Orchestra three years ago because *The Maningpool Telegraph* has at times had occasion to attack his performances, needless to say in a purely professional and impersonal spirit.

Noel Robert Clanricarde Grampian was born on December 25, 1887, at Rowlington, Gloamshire. He came of fairly humble middle-class parentage, his father having been an official at Rowlington Council House. Both his parents were musical, his mother having been a not unsuccessful local singer before her marriage. It was she, indeed, who introduced him to the rudiments of music and taught him the piano during what was almost his babyhood. Later he learnt a great deal from George Tilleyard, organist of Elswater Parish Church, Rowlington, where he sang in the choir until his voice broke. He then came to Maningpool School of Music—his first association with our City, for which he always retained an abiding affection during his musical wanderings, as he was never tired of confessing.

On completing his education at Maningpool, he became organist and choirmaster at St. Peter's Church, Inclevale, a post he abandoned, however, for a travelling life that was more congenial to his artistic temperament, as conductor of the now extinct Thomas Hilkington Opera Company. Here he gained much valuable experience, although the repertoire consisted mainly of popular operas of the lighter type, and during a visit to Harmsford-on-Sea, where the now famous orchestra was about to be formed, he so much impressed some of those in authority with his vivid conducting that he was engaged forthwith to take charge of the new organisation. This nearly involved him in an action for breach of contract, no doubt undeservedly, and he not only conducted the Harmsford Orchestra from 1920 until 1931 with unvarying success, but made it, by persistent work and artistic endeavour, into a far finer body of players than had originally been contemplated by its founders. It was through his efforts that what had been intended to be merely a good seaside orchestra, capable of adequately entertaining the public, became competent to give a fortnightly Symphony Concert of excellent quality.

In 1931, unfortunately, a quarrel with the Municipality led to the resignation of Mr. Grampian (as he then was), a step he was induced to take, it was said, by the opposition of one particular member of the Committee. He then undertook a tour in Australia and New Zealand, where he conducted the resident orchestras in a manner which the overseas Press repeatedly lauded as sensationally striking, and he did, in particular, much excellent work on behalf of living British composers, a service for which he well deserved the knighthood conferred on him on his return at the end of 1934.

It was in September, 1935, as "Maningpudlians" must well remember, that Sir Noel Grampian took charge of the Municipal Orchestra, and his subsequent biography is well known to all readers of *The Maningpool Telegraph*. Sir Noel, it is less generally known, since Lady Grampian has never lived in this City, married Miss Laetitia Parkings, a younger sister of Mrs. Humphrey Gillighan, the wife of the Professor of Music at Maningpool

University. It adds not a little to last night's tragedy that Mrs. Gillighan should have played second harp in the orchestra, as she always has done since her marriage whenever an extra instrument of the kind was required.

Note: It has been thought inadvisable to publish a notice of last night's Symphony Concert, which was so disastrously interrupted; but our musical critic, J. R., has been asked to contribute his impressions of the circumstances of Sir Noel Grampian's death to his "Musical Notes" column on Monday next.—ED.

Saturday, 1st October

FOUR GEORGES HOTEL,
MANINGPOOL.

1. X. 38.

MY DEAR JULIA,

This can go off to you to-night, though I may have something more to write about to-morrow, in which case you'll get the two lots on Monday morning. I shall register all the documents I send you, and I know, of course, that you'll be silent as the grave about them and lock them up in the safe immediately you have read them. Any comments from you will be as welcome as ever—more so, perhaps, because your musical knowledge may help.

My own letters are more in the nature of a *soulagement* on my part, and I shall never want to see them again in all their redundance. But they do always help me in mentally pigeonholing the outstanding ideas afterwards with the aid of short notes, and eventually piecing them together—I hope and pray—into a pattern. But it's the very deuce of a case.

At the outset there were over 2,000 suspects—a record, you'll admit. However, the audience is definitely eliminated, as nobody could have inflicted that particular wound from behind Grampian, and you will have gathered from yesterday's cuttings that nobody escaped from the hall after the death, thanks to the locals' presence of mind in having the doors closed immediately. (I make a reservation, though: after the *death*, yes; but what about after the *shot*? There was a lapse of perhaps half a minute between the two, and you can get a long way in thirty seconds—you try!) The orchestra alone, then, is really under suspicion, and quite enough, too. However, I agree with the people here—nice chap, the Chief Constable, and an efficient staff—that the considerable number of casual players specially engaged for that concert on account of the huge orchestra required by Strauss, some from London and elsewhere, others resident musicians who either like to turn an additional penny (comparatively honest, I suppose) or who enjoy taking part as amateurs (like Beatrice), may be eliminated, at any rate for the moment. Both the Police and the Orchestra Secretary have their addresses, needless to say.

The permanent members are another matter. As far as I can see, every one of them may have a motive, if N. G. was half the bounder I understand him to have been, and about 50 percent of them, if not more, could have shot him, considering that, impossible as it seems on the face of it that *anyone* did, he actually and incontrovertibly *was* shot. (I'll come back to the notion of suicide presently.)

You've seen the account of the death: the "eye-witness" puts it all quite usefully, and, I gather from the Police, who have questioned countless others, accurately. There remains the nature of the injury, though, and the interval between the shot and death. Well, the Police surgeon, Dr. Belham, gave me the facts (or conjectures?) in the usual rather aggrieved and "needless-to-say" manner. It appears that the bullet entered the body in an almost horizontal line and just a little from the left, and touched the base of the heart, a fleshy part, not one of the tubes and gadgets (forgive the non-technical translation of what, true to his kind, the doctor delighted in keeping as professionally obscure as possible). From what I can make out, such a heart wound is not, so to speak, directly lethal, but produces a convulsion that amounts to a deadly kind of stroke. This comes quickly, but not necessarily immediately. It is thus quite possible that Grampian not only lived for some seconds—between 10 and 30, perhaps— after the shot, but could actually go on beating time, or at any rate brandishing his stick jerkily (*vide* Press) when he had already been shot. Furthermore, he might have been actually killed by the fall on his head, not in the first place by the shot, though that was of course the direct cause of the fall, and he must have been pretty far gone not to have instinctively put out his hands to break the fall.

Anyway, we have a possible lapse of time between the shot and the moment of death, which means, mark you, the *discovery* of death, during which a murderer might have got away before the doors were closed. But if so, where did he come from? If the shot could have been fired only from the orchestra, he did not escape, for all the players were still there and underwent a detailed verbal examination from the locals. Were they searched? you'll ask, as I did. They were not. The offending weapon, a neat little revolver, lay on the platform for all to see, in front of the leader of the violas and not far from N. G. himself, who might have dropped it after committing suicide *coram populo*. Only he didn't, for the shot had clearly come from some distance, otherwise his beautiful boiled shirt-front would have been badly scorched. Also, the doctor opined, the shot would have penetrated farther and been aimed higher, let alone the fact that its angle was unconvincing. It's a pity, rather, that this theory goes by the board, for N. G.

seems to have been a spectacular sort of Johnny—you should hear Humphrey and Beatrice about him—and such a gesture in the middle of a performance would have been magnificently in character. And I think "A Hero's Life" would have been precisely the work in the course of which he would have chosen to vanish in a final puff of glory.

The weapon, a pretty toy, was fully loaded, and one shot had been fired not long ago. A matter of minutes at the most. They smelt it. Good enough, I suppose. Anyhow, *they* supposed so. The thing is now at the central Police Station, together with the bullet retrieved by Dr. Belham from the body. The two fit, but have not been examined by an expert. The Chief Constable here doesn't believe in labouring the obvious, nor do I in the present instance; and if it should cease to be obvious, we can soon get the exhibits up to the Yard.

You may wonder whether all these suspects just go about their daily round as usual or whether they have all been incarcerated. Or am I doing you an injustice? I'm sure I am. They are all at large, of course, and there is no chief suspect at the moment, for we all refuse to believe that the viola leader is more likely to be our chap because the revolver lay in front of him. Murderers don't advertise themselves quite so flagrantly. Moreover, it lay in front of quite a lot of people, even though at different distances, and if you are going to chuck a revolver away from you after a shot, you may as well hurl it ten yards as ten inches. So they are all at liberty, but continue to report on rehearsal days, three times a week, as usual, although of course no rehearsals are held. If anyone should be missing, he will have revealed himself as almost certainly guilty, and it won't be very difficult to get him, as nobody in the orchestra, the Sec. assures us, is ever in sufficient funds to take him far. They are not too well paid, they receive their salaries weekly, and most of them are in the habit of asking for advances at various times.

Go on, ask about fingerprints! Not a sign, or hardly a one. So your next question, prompted by me, must be how a man in full view of an audience of 2,000 can not only fire a shot unobserved and fling his weapon down on the ground, but calmly wipe off fingerprints between these two performances. The answer is that he didn't. The revolver is obligingly covered with a criss-cross pattern of the kind that not only prevents its slipping between the shooter's fingers, but makes an examination of prints impossible. *Voilà!* Or rather not *voilà*, for there is something more. An almost microscopic examination showed that the little tiny embossed, lozenge-shaped shields raised between the crissings and crossings (if that's the description) show on their surfaces of less than a square millimetre any number of traces of prints; but they are so broken up by the aforesaid crossings and crissings as to refuse obstinately to fall into any sort of pattern. The only thing observed, negatively and quite uncertainly, is that somehow they do not seem to make any continuity, as though the revolver had been touched by several hands, each leaving its most accentuated marks in different places.

That should give you enough to knit your adorable brows over for a start. Think of me while you execute this most enchanting bit of needlework, won't you? And if you know who the murderer is, tell me at once. I want to arrest him and come home. Oh Lord!

I'll write again to-morrow, when I shall have been to lunch with the Gillighans. Beatrice says I must come *every Sunday* as long as I'm here. She at any rate has no illusions about my being able to solve this case in a hurry. Or has she? Perhaps she thinks that standing invitation is quite safe because I'm bound to catch the culprit in less than a month of Sundays. I don't know. I just don't know anything whatsoever. If it weren't for the babes, I'd resign, I think. Love them much for me.

Yours for aye,

ALAN.

Sunday, 2nd October

FOUR GEORGES,
MANINGPOOL.

Sunday morning.

DARLING JU,

How good early Oct. can be in England, even three hours north of London! This is one of those days of weather-clerkly (or is it weather-clerical?) repentance for sins committed during the summer. I arrived here in a Cimmerian gloom on Friday morning, by no means dispelled by the dismal happenings at the Civic Hall, and this morning I woke up feeling, somehow, that they can't possibly have taken place or alternatively, I'm afraid, that the world is none the worse for the providential removal of Sir N. G. I am beginning to wonder whether I'm not interfering unwarrantably in trying to bring the instrument of a wiser order of things than we know of before the representatives of a more fallible human justice. But who is a Horfficer of the Lor to talk thus? Still, it's a relief to do so to thee, O Wife, and only one more token of my trust in thee.

Also, it is evidence of my having nothing to think about but idle chatter. The fact is that I have been deliberately shutting out all speculation ever since last night. I want to clear myself of all first impressions for a bit and see what comes into my mind without my bidding. As you know, it has worked quite usefully before now.

I like this town in many ways, and you really ought, as Beatrice never ceases to remark, to follow my example and visit the Gillighan ménage one day. Not that I should have done so had it not been for last week's professional excursion to this county. Ah, would you were here now! Or do I? I couldn't write to you then, that would be the snag. Should I have to keep a diary? No, no, not that!

But as I say, the aforementioned ménage is pleasant, at any rate as to its exterior. It's true that Beatrice is never tired of saying that Humphrey has been unbearable, exasperating, intolerable, and what not; but as she always says it in front of him, I fancy there's not much in it. My impression is that he is rather suffocatingly devoted to her whenever he does not happen to be wholly absorbed in preparing a lecture or studying a score or editing and transcribing an old MS., at which moments he seems to be completely oblivious of her existence. Then again, he'd do absolutely anything for her, with a sort of unquestioning adoration that may be rather a bore. But I don't pretend to understand it. I can't say I worship her gushy-wushy and "aren't-I-sweet" type myself. However, I'm spoilt. (Don't blush!) Humphrey isn't: it's he who does the spoiling. Rather absurd and a little pathetic.

The house is delightful. Very early Victoria, or even William IV, I should say. A drawing-room four French windows long taking up all one side of the ground-floor, with a trellised veranda running all along outside overgrown with what ought to be wistaria if it isn't actually. (On second thoughts, it must be, for Beatrice always does the proper and expected thing.) It overlooks a lawn with a mulberry tree in the centre. The dining-room and a sort of sitting-room-study adaptable to various occasions are on the road side, where there is a largish front garden with a drive going round a circular bed occupied by tubby box trees cut into different squat shapes. The real study, though, full of books on music, scores, complete editions of the musical classics, and so on, is upstairs, a lovely, sunny den on the garden side next to the principal bedroom. My room last week was at the side of the house with a rather grand view over the town from the heights of Rookdale. (Why "dale" I don't know.) I confess I am looking forward to a little luxury, though I'm really comfortable here and refuse all Beatrice's blandishments to return to the Gillighanry, much to her manifest surprise, for she is accustomed to regarding herself as irresistible. I fancy she puts it all down to the hard policeman streak in me. Poor thing, she must explain it to herself somehow.

This hotel is very central, almost as much so as the Langdon, which is the new station hotel, just opened, I hear, by the Lord Mayor of M'pool in full municipal panoply; a pretentious palace of a very white local stone, like an erection made of newly fallen snow about to melt into the surrounding grime. Buildings more than a year old are pretty black here, with something of the fine velvety sootiness of Portland stone, but without its startling high lights. There's nothing like London—says the Londoner who is out of it. I'm not aware that I ever look at it when I'm there.

M'pool is an agreeable surprise in some ways, seeing that it has long been a stock music-hall joke. It is drab, certainly, but somehow spacious, big-towny, and in several places almost Continental: a big restaurant with stained glass windows with a German touch of home-from-home comfort-cum-fugginess, a travel agent's with a boulevard-like look about it, a motor-car show-room as vast and ornate as a mosque—all this in or near the huge square in front of the central station and its snow palace, a really fine expanse with a group of statuary and a fountain in the middle, yet with the English provincial reluctance to be pictur-esque. The one dispirited flower-woman, a newspaper kiosk that looks half ashamed of its outlandishness (though it's anything but Turkish), and a couple of half-hearted electric signs at night, one of them perpetually lighting a cigarette at short intervals— all rather jolly, but self-conscious and just not quite genuine. Park Street, the main shopping street, is good enough, very wide and full of clanging trams and agitated buses bearing quite common names of destinations that are yet strange to me. I picture all these suburbs in directions that are quite definitely settled in my mind, yet found to be entirely elsewhere when I look at the map of the town in the hotel vestibule. I thought I'd long ago given up preconceiving anything. Well, one still lives and still learns, and anyhow nobody could accuse me of having any pre- or other conception of my present case. Apart from that, my fixed ideas about the suburbs seem to indicate that I've got any amount of imagination (ahem!).

But I must go. The call of Beatrice may be resistible, but not that of her admirable table.

Sunday night.

Here we are again. Listen, love. There was nobody else at the G.s', rather to my surprise. Beatrice seems to have momentarily exhausted her passion for getting people to meet each other. So we had a heart-to-hearter about sister Letty, who, by the way, not only refused to live with her husband, but has even declined to attend his funeral, which takes place to-morrow. She will, however, come to stay with the G.s presently, it appears, now that the coast is clear. Unless my case goes much more quickly than I dare to expect, I shall doubtless see her, and I admit I could bear to do so. Meanwhile I have had some distinctly interesting information, imparted with considerable heat by Beatrice, and by Humphrey with a sort of half-amused indignation that gradually, under B.'s influence, grew into something more like chivalrous wrath coupled with, I thought, a certain embarrassment due probably to an obscure consciousness that he was being got at by his adored wife in front of me and made to say more than he really felt. He has an odd streak of shyness in him. Or am I being too subtle?

The long and the short of it all is that Grampian and his wife got on quite well at first, after their marriage at Harmsford, where of course the Parkings girls came from, as you know. Beatrice has told me a good deal about their early days there: old Parkings was a prosperous business man of sorts, a Londoner, who had retired rather early on account of bad health and settled at Harmsford for its supposedly good air, which has always seemed to me to be a judiciously perpetuated myth, the advantages of a very pleasant winter only occasionally interrupted by some arctic blasts being completely nullified by an insupportably stifling and relaxing summer.

But this is neither here nor there—certainly not here, where the delightful weather to-day does not interfere with the admirably bracing atmosphere of the place. Well, Miss Laetitia Parkings, not very long after her transformation into Mrs. Noel

Grampian, began to be aware of a subtle deterioration in her husband's manners—always precarious and subject to the influence of moods, as the G.s say—and to find that his attentions began to wander from her personal attractions, which I understand to be considerable, in the direction of those of other ladies—and not always strictly speaking ladies—who may not have had the advantage of being better looking, but in the nature of things had that of being different. Who was it said of Don Juan that his delight was "not in the woman but the chase"? But what is even truer of that gentleman, as well as of N.G., so far as he had it in him to emulate such a grandee, is "not in the woman but in change." After some minor episodes, a major scandal or two brought matters to a head, and Letty went home to mother and father, refusing with any amount of spirit, not only to have the least thing to do with her husband, but also to oblige him with the divorce for which he had placed any amount of material at her disposal. Beatrice is, of course, loyal to her sister and was careful not to let her down, but I gathered all the same that Letty's reason for taking up this obstinate attitude was much less any hope of winning the undesirable creature back to herself eventually than simply to annoy him by as much chicanery as may be compatible with the behaviour of a perfect lady—and I have learnt that it can be quite a respectable amount.

The serio-comic, and to Humphrey rather amusing, sequel was—and it was he who took the lead here in relating the story and probing for motives—that N.G., true to his kind, didn't really at all mind not being let off by his wife. He felt, no doubt, that his enforced grass-widowerhood would still leave him plenty of margin for enjoying himself in his own fashion, and save him at the same time from any possibility of having to put a matrimonial finish to any of his exploits, as he would almost certainly have been forced to do in one of his Harmsford cases. There were some pretty influential people at Harmsford, and I rather gathered that he might easily have poached all too rashly on their feminine preserves. It wasn't anything the G.s said, but I felt that there was a certain significance in their sudden anxiety to change the conversation when I hinted that the opposition of one particular member of the Harmsford Orchestra Committee seemed to me suggestive. Their silence only confirms my suspicion, and it is worth remembering that when a committee decides to get rid of a man it has appointed, there is as a rule some purely professional or business reason for such a step if it does so in a body or by the pressure of a majority, but a purely personal reason when one single member moves the dismissal and manages to persuade the rest to act on his motion.

I should have liked to insist on more information, but could not, as the G.s' guest, very well press the point when I began to sense reluctance on their part; and it was very clear that Beatrice is most ardently devoted to her younger sister and has been living in an almost frantic state of distress about that unhappy marriage. Humphrey, in fact, told me when we were alone that the whole thing had made his wife positively ill, and it is only too plain that this in turn has been a constant source of worry to himself.

With the M'pool Orchestra Grampian was scarcely more popular than with his in-laws. It seems that the players had actually gone to the length of pleading for his removal. Humphrey, as you may know, is Chairman of the Committee, and he tells me that just before the new season started, after they had had the first three or four rehearsals, a deputation consisting of the leader and of the principals of each instrumental group formally approached Humphrey with a petition that N. G. should be sacked. They called on him and he saw them "in this very room"—we were sitting over a glass of sherry in his quasi-study next to the dining-room before lunch while Beatrice was putting the finishing touches either to the meal or to herself, I don't know which, but both were exceedingly finished. She does know how to keep house, and she is, of course, in her way a charming woman, as indeed any friend of yours could not fail to be, with her masses of fuzzy, ashen hair parted in the middle and her wide, aggressively frank and yet somehow cat-like, inscrutable grey eyes. Well, I'm afraid I prefer brown, smooth hair, parted at the side, a smaller, less statuesque but equally shapely figure, and eyes the colour of which I have never yet been able to describe—and so much more lastingly loved and admired for that. Do you recognise the like-ness? If so, give her lots of my love. Also to her adorable children, which I am not sorry to confess happen to be also mine.

Ever and ever yours,

ALAN.

Monday, 3rd October

FOUR GEORGES HOTEL,
MANINGPOOL.

3. x. 38.

DEAREST JULIA,

Do read the enclosed, which appeared in this morning's local rag—or rather the better of the two local rags, though the other may be the tougher one. It's not uninteresting, I think, though I'm hanged if I understand the jargon with which you musicians insist on surrounding your precious art. Do I sound peevish? I don't mean to. But this thing is a bit nerve-racking. I'm dealing with about 60 suspects, at the very least, even if I do eliminate, as I'm inclined to, all the temporary players marked on the list of the orchestra I enclose for your delectation. For the moment I really can't face considering these casuals as well as the regulars. Well, I've come to the conclusion that I can't possibly interview them all (the latter), so, to start with, I've asked the Sec. to get them all to write out statements for me, telling me details of their careers, of their engagement in M'pool and, if they have any, their ideas about the slaughter. I'll see what comes of it and then begin to talk to those I think suspicious. I hope, that is, their letters will weed out a good many of them straight off—I don't quite know how, but I can only feel my way and trust a bit to psychology, horrified though Higgy would be at the bare idea. I'll send you the stuff I get from them, or copies. Also anything else that crops up. See what you can make of it, if you will, in case a musical point arises that eludes me. I've never felt such a fool in my life. Five dozen suspects and a case touching a field in which I walk about like a blind man in a bog. Help!

Many hugs to the children and to yourself.

Ever yours,

ALAN.

P.S. Taplow, the Sec., has also offered to make me a sketch-plan of the seating of the orch. I'll trace you a copy when it comes. But don't puzzle too much over the case. It's overwhelming!

Cutting from *The Maningpool Telegraph*

MUSICAL NOTES

SIR NOEL GRAMPIAN'S DEATH
Possible Clues from the Score

The murder of Sir Noel Grampian on Thursday last is still haunting the public mind and exercising the police, including, it is now generally known, Detective-Inspector Alan Hope of Scotland Yard. We may no doubt confidently leave these highly experienced officers to their intricate work; but there can be no harm in our indulging in some mild speculations of our own, if we happen to be interested in the musical aspect of the case. For it has occurred to me that it undoubtedly does present a musical aspect, and I cannot help thinking that, police officials not being as a rule trained musicians—which on the whole may be just as well for the safety of us all—those of us who happen to know something about music may possibly help the professional investigators by a little amateurish sleuthing. For my part, I am convinced that without a study of the score of Strauss's "Heldenleben," no solution of the mystery can be profitably attempted. I will try to show my reasons for this view.

Let us glance at the score at the point where the music broke off on Thursday—that is to say, where Sir Noel was killed. I was following the performance closely with the score, and to the best of my recollection the music began to become unsettled on page 153 of the miniature score, just after the cue number 79 which appears over the first bar on that page. I may say that I saw nothing of what was happening until the conductor had actually crashed to the floor—mercifully for me—and it will be understood that as soon as I found that the music was going to pieces, I naturally looked at the score all the more closely, in order to check what was going wrong. For several bars things did go from bad to worse, and holes began to appear conspicuously in the harmonic texture, where players who happened to be looking at the conductor saw him staggering and left off, while others, of course, who had their eyes on their music at the moment, played on for a few bars. The actual break occurred, to the best of my recollection, on page 154, where the music modulates from E flat major to B major, but just before the signature of the latter key is established at cue number 80 on page 155.

I do not know what the medical evidence is: whether Sir Noel was first killed by the shot or by his fall, or whether each accelerated the effect of the other, I am not competent to decide. But it seems to me evident that he was wounded with an immediately mortal effect, for a man does not continue to conduct if he has only been gravely hurt, nor does he on the other hand collapse so suddenly in the middle of his work unless his injury causes death without delay. Any lighter injury would have caused Sir Noel to stop conducting abruptly, but not to fall immediately, if at all. It follows that not more than a few seconds can have elapsed between the shot and Sir Noel's fall.

Here we come upon the question of the inaudibility of the shot, which has caused so much surprise. We can guess from the nature of Sir Noel's collapse, unless I am wildly mistaken, pretty accurately at what moment of the performance it was fired. But why was it not heard? Dismissing fantastic detective-story notions of silent pistols and the rest, we are forced to come to the conclusion that a considerable amount of noise must have been going on to cover up the shot. But although several parts after cue 79 are marked *fff* by Strauss, the texture there is comparatively sparse and the effect not what one would call noisy, nor is the approach to the climax on page 152 nearly so clamorous as the infernal din of the "Battle" section, which has reached its end some ten pages earlier. That section, with its ceaseless beating of drums, one would have thought, was the part of the work to be chosen by a murderer who wished to remain undetected, and who might perhaps have calculated on firing an unheard shot not quite so immediately deadly as that which killed Sir Noel. On pages 152-3 the loud *tutti* passages are not supported by drums or any other percussion, which always means not only a nobler, less rowdy sort of loudness, but a kind of sound through which such a crash as that of a revolver report would be sure to penetrate.

But stay! Talking of crashes, there is after all just one percussion effect in the passage with which we are concerned—a cymbal clash reinforcing the very accentuated and widespread E flat major chord on the first beat at cue 79. And that hissing sound, combined with the loudness of the chord, would drown almost anything. I submit, therefore, for what the idea may be worth to the detectives engaged upon the case of this incredible murder, that this was the exact moment at which the fatal shot was fired at Sir Noel Grampian.

It is not for me to speculate by whom it was done, and I do not pretend to know, not being able to say with the buccaneers bold of Scotland Yard that "crime's my chief delight"; but a study of the score does suggest that there are only a limited number of possibilities, which these highly skilled gentlemen, if they can read music, may be able to sort out for themselves. If the shot was really fired at cue 79, it is a simple matter to find out from the score which of the players happened to be busy at that moment.

J. R.

Page from the Symphony Concert

Programme, 29th September 1938

THE MANINGPOOL MUNICIPAL ORCHESTRA

(Players marked * have been specially engaged for the performance of "A Hero's Life"; those marked † are giving their services voluntarily.)

First Violins

Eltham, C. (Leader)

Holcombe, F. J.

Ricksworth, W. W.

Bell, T.

Bowington, K. O.

Lark, Miss D.

Helper, J.

Doyle, Miss C.

*Lollington, G. W.

† Barker, I. P.

† Benbridge, Mrs. A.

† Nestling, Miss H.

Second Violins

Grant, F. D. (Principal)

Temple, F.

Trimmington, J. L.

Gellings, L. P.

Griffith, Ll. E.

Rambotham, J. J.

Labouchère, F.

Elsworth, Miss K.

*Ettington, Miss F.

†Barbidge, G. W.

Violas

Dashwood, T. W. (Principal)

Oostermans, G.

Gough, R. B.

Crawley, S. R.

Morgan, T. D.

Lamb, Miss R.

*Bard, H. G.

†Terry, Miss G.

Violoncellos

Deenery, W. G. (Principal)

Doyle, E. B.

Cohen, A.

Zimmermann, K.

Eastern, G. F.

Damper, O. H.

†Trampington, Mrs. J.

†Carlton, L. J.

Double Basses

Thirsfeld, F. J. (Principal)

Phillips, E.

Spinney, W. J.

Barnes, T.

*Osborn, L. B.

*Northfield, M. M.

Piccolo

Repton, A. M.

Flutes

Beckenham, R. S.

Alsworthy, J. W.

†Impney, F.

Oboes

Simmons, K. H.

Best, F. M.

*Tilling, F.

Cor Anglais
Lovelock, G.

Clarinets
Evans, B.
Potter, F.

E flat Clarinet
*Bluffer, M. F.

Bass Clarinet
Ashton, G.

Bassoons
Tufton, D. M.
Blandford, J. G.
*Gill, T.

Double Bassoon
Arlington, O.

Horns
Stillingham, W. J.
Bansted, G.
Bettering, F. J.
Hurnd, J.
*Arling, D. S.
*Rackstraw, H. W.
*Rasmussen, H.
*Starkey, D. G.

Trumpets
Holborne, F. H.
Beardling, M.

Gorton, H. M.
*Repp, D.
*Grippling, S. S.

Trombones
Mere, P. G.
Cook, G. H.
Chalmers, E.

Tenor Tuba
*Still, E. F.

Bass Tuba
Rompton, H.

Harps
Jarvis, Miss G.
†Gillighan, Mrs. B.

Percussion
Dipton, F. S. (Timpani)
Mills, T. M.
Franklin, E. G.
*Lorman, J. J.
*Smith, W. G.

Tuesday, 4th October

FOUR GEORGES HOTEL,

MANINGPOOL.

4. X. 38.

DEAREST JU,

No developments yet. But I forgot to say yesterday that I asked Ransom to see me (J. R. of the *M'pool Telegraph*, you know), which he can't do till to-morrow evening, as he's gone to London on some professional jaunt. He expects us—the Police, if you please!—to read full scores. Well, well! Kindly apply to Mr. Philo Vance and other omniscients of the imaginary world of detection. I shall have to confess to him that this is not among my accomplishments, at the risk of disillusioning him for ever and earning his eternal scorn. Fortunately for me, perhaps, none of the Police people here knows any better than I do, and they have not even got musical wives, which is where I have the advantage of them.

But Ransom's idea that the list of possible suspects can be drastically reduced appeals to me vastly, you won't be surprised to hear. So I'm going to make him do a spot of serious work (which will be a change for a musical critic) and puzzle out for me with the help of his precious score what he can make of those limited possibilities of his. I fancy we shall get some fun out of each other's ignorance of each other's jobs, and let's hope we may both learn something too. *If* he's teachable, which I doubt.

Critics must never admit that there may be a thing or two they don't know. J. R. at any rate, is a proper layer down of laws. Well, as long as there are musical people in the world, their laws must, I suppose, be laid down for them by somebody. I wonder what Ransom is going to be like as a person. He sounds grand over the telephone.

Love to the lot of you,

ALAN.

COTSWOLDS COTTAGE,

59 ARDEN ROAD,

MANINGPOOL, 14.

3rd October, 1938.

Private and Confidential.

DEAR SIR,

You may have read, and possibly been impressed by, my colleague's article, in this morning's issue of *The Maningpool Telegraph*. It seems to me, however, if I may say so, somewhat in the nature of an ingenious fabrication. It is, perhaps, an impertinence on my part, to write to you, without further reflection; but, *Nunc aut nunquam*, if I may quote my old School device (I was at Uptonborough), for all that J. R., who has not had that privilege, would, doubtless, sneer at such a classical allusion.

It has occurred to me, that I could, perhaps, throw a little more light on the tragic death of my excellent friend, our great, and much-admired, *Musensohn*, than J. R. has been able to do in a column of print. I do not presume to be able to teach you your business, but "the onlooker sees most of the game," and, not only do I understand, that you were not present at last Thursday's concert, but I can assert that J. R. can have seen nothing whatever, as, according to his wont, he had his nose buried in the score. *Honni soit, qui mal y pense,* perhaps, but I am bound to say that, possibly, the *Telegraph* would have been able to publish fairer estimates of the late Sir Noel's wonderful art, if their critic had looked at the great conductor a little more closely. But, in spite of the special opportunity given him, he utterly failed to appreciate that unique genius.

If you should desire a short interview, perhaps you would kindly ring me at my house, (Gimpling, 3572), some time to-morrow morning, when I shall be very glad to call on you, at your convenience. I suggest this, in preference to asking you here, because this house is somewhat far out, and I, in any case, look in almost daily at the office of *The Maningpool Messenger.* (You know, doubtless, that I am attached to that journal, as musical critic.)

Believe me,

Yours very truly,
FREDERICK M. LORWOOD.

DETECTIVE-INSPECTOR A. HOPE,
    THE FOUR GEORGES HOTEL,
        MANINGPOOL.

Here's something else for you, darling: it came in this morning, after I had written to you about Ransom, whom I am quite beginning to like, after the enclosed! I'll see that pompous ass Lorwood to-day, if only for the fun of it. He'll tell me, in rather less than so many words, that Ransom shot N. G., I shouldn't wonder. But I verily believe he's himself the murderer. No man who uses so many superfluous commas can be innocent. Or is that merely the Uptonborough touch? I've a good mind to tell him I know a man who was there: Charlie Blandson, you know; and then, when he has begun to beam all over, let him know about C. B.'s disgraceful swindles. I know you hope I shan't. Julia, goddess of good breeding, succour me!

Later:

He's been, gone, seen, been seen, and has not conquered. What a specimen! He's as full of proverbs as Sancho Panza, as great a fool and very considerably less human. But see for yourself in the enclosed notice of N. G.'s first symphony concert. Isn't it a gem? He quoted several German titles, apart from "Heldenleben," and a number of French *mots* at me. I don't quite know about the former, but the latter were doubly offensive, first because of an incredible *Uppe-ton-bourg* accent and secondly because of his bland assumption that a policeman doesn't know French from frangipane.

Yes, he was most entertainingly poisonous about Ransom, while he assumed a kind of gentleman's forbearance *vis-à-vis* (as he would say) a caddish upstart who is not utterly devoid of a certain veneer of cleverness and has to be politely tolerated by a man of the world into whose profession he has gate-crashed. That sort of thing. At the same time he managed to convey to me, who knows nothing about that profession, that he himself is a duffer, whereas I cannot help gathering that Ransom is gifted in some way.

Well, it appears that Ransom was sitting in a place right at the side of the gallery, entirely by himself, nobody having come with him to occupy his second complimentary seat. (Hint No. 1.) But, no doubt in a spirit of contradiction, he had refused to look at N. G. and buried his head in the scores of all the music done in the first part of the programme as well as in that of "Heldenleben," deliberately refraining from looking up for so much as a second. (Hint No. 2.) And dear Sir Noel had been more wonderfully alive and mobile than ever that night, and turned continually from side to side in order to induce this or that group of players to make their points with the utmost eloquence. (Hint No. 3: do you see it?)

What did Lorwood's suggestions about the murder, and his refutation of Ransom's suggestions, amount to? Well, precisely nothing at all. It was all merely important wind-baggery, and I saw pretty soon that all he had come for (assuming charitably that he had not consciously done so to throw suspicion on Ransom) was to chuck his weight about, to show how much more impressive he is than Ransom (all because of an inferiority complex bred by his writing for an inferior paper), to find another person whom he could tell how well he has known that great man Sir Noel Grampian (and I have no doubt he has known him much better since last Thursday) and lastly to press that cutting of his notice into my hand in order to let me judge, as he modestly put it, what Grampian was really like as a conductor, since, he added, he should not like me to obtain a warped impression from J. R.'s perverse and ill-natured judgment, due to the fact, he had no doubt, that he did not enjoy the privilege of N. G.'s friendship. All I do judge, however, is that the Maningpudlian dialect of journalese seems to be the most offensive. Another illusion gone: I thought music critics were paid to write about music.

And so to bed, my love. Sleep well, and I hope the kids are doing so already.

Just one more stroke to my thumb-nail sketch: F. M. L. prefaced his footling conjectures about the murder, which I have mercifully spared you, with the remark that J. R.'s reference to "mild speculations" in his article yesterday had doubtless been a misprint for "wild speculations."

Cutting from *The Maningpool Messenger*
Friday, 16th September 1938

BRILLIANT FIRST SYMPHONY CONCERT
SIR NOEL GRAMPIAN'S TRIUMPHANT RETURN
Galaxy of Fashion and Talent

It was an elegant and intelligent Maningpool, that assembled at the always impressive Civic Hall, for the season's first Symphony Concert, last night. In the more expensive stalls, and the centre of the dress-circle, sat rows upon rows of well-dressed, eager members of the City's more substantial Society, in serried ranks, and, indeed, if so vulgar an expression were not fantastically out of place, almost cheek by jowl. One could not help reflecting thankfully that Maningpool has not yet, like so many other provincial towns, relinquished the gracious garb of evening dress, at such functions as these; and all those who have the dignity and good form of the best elements of the City at heart, cannot but ardently wish that this state of affairs will prevail, as long as the British

Empire itself shall last, indeed as long as Art will endure; and Art is longer not only than Life, but even, if possible, than Empires.

Our music-lovers' attention, at these concerts, has always been a matter for congratulation and wonder. Only here and there, does a member of the audience, quite inadvertently, one has no doubt, have the ill-luck to arrive a few moments late; but we are not here, as Hamlet said, the City's "tardy son to chide," and the suggestion, that was recently made by the musical critic of our contemporary, that late-comers should be kept waiting in the corridors, even if the opening work should be a whole, long Symphony, strikes one as nothing less than monstrous. After all, he who pays the piper, not only calls the tune, but is most assuredly entitled to hear the tune, and the whole tune.

But this merely by way of *hors-d'oeuvre*. The event of the evening was, of course, the reappearance of the Maningpool Municipal Orchestra, and especially, none but Envy itself will gainsay it, the return of Maningpool's great conductor, so truly Maningpool's own already, after but three years of activity here. This was—can one hesitate to say it?—the event, not only of the evening, but of the Season, nay, of the year, as only a musical disbelieving Thomas could deny. What is more, those of us, who have the privilege of enjoying Sir Noel's personal friendship, are well aware how happy he is, too, to be once more among us, and to commence again, dispensing music from that bottomless cornucopia of his genius.

No doubt, as in his modesty, which is the modesty ever allied to true artistry, he would be the last to deny, something must be booked to the credit of the composers who made up last night's programme by three great Symphonies. But it was, perhaps,

Sir Noel's cunning juxtaposition of these three masterpieces, between which there is nothing to choose in greatness (for a musical Paris would have found it impossible to decide to which of these three beauties the prize should be awarded): Mozart's Symphony in G minor, Schubert's "Unfinished Symphony," and Tschaikowsky's Fifth Symphony; it was that cunning juxtaposition, one repeats, which was the most remarkable feature of a programme in itself a veritable *embarras de richesses*. Here, indeed, was an Epicurean feast, but a feast made wholly delectable only by the hand that had so faultlessly devised it.

And then, how perfectly cooked it was! Sir Noel will take no offence at this comparison, purely momentary, of his supreme art to the very minor one of the *cuisine*, for, after all, do not the French call a conductor their *chef d'orchestre*? Where is one to begin, describing the art with which a Grampian wields the *bâton*? (Here, again, one makes no apology for this bald use of the Knight's surname, for that is how Sir Noel will be known to posterity: as Grampian, just Grampian, as one says Milton, Michelangelo, or Molesworthy; and our regional Poet is brought in here advisedly, not for the sake of alliteration, but because he, too, as his friends know full well, is among the elect.) Where begin, indeed, where all is, as Carlyle remarked, "significant of much"? It is a question, rather of ending without undue abruptness, for space will not permit even a modest tithe of discussion of all those fascinating details, on which one might expound.

Suffice it to say, then, that under the hands of Sir Noel great music becomes greater. The gentle, graceful Mozart for the nonce becomes almost exciting, Schubert's homely phrases acquire a new passion, and even Tschaikowsky (whose name is persistently mis-spelt by our contemporary) gains in force and poignancy. Whatever Sir Noel touches, with those daring, pouncing, immensely vital and mobile methods of his, seems to grow in stature and to shine with a new light—even to the greatest—until one aches to cry to him: *Lumen soli mutuum das.*

F. M. L.

Wednesday, 5th October

FOUR GEORGES.

5. X. 38.

(IN FACT NEARLY 6. X. 38.)

DEAR ONE,

Here's a copy of the news I had from Ailner—hideously confidential, of course. But you know how I trust you, and even so I am able to let you see this only because no vital names are mentioned. He's a good man and had been quick at the job. Grampian's goings-on at Harmsford are interesting, distinctly, and they do throw light on his character—a far from savoury character. Ransom tells me, by the way, that the orch. used to call him N. G. when they happened to feel relatively affectionate towards him, which was—what, never? well, hardly ever—and N. B. G. otherwise. They disesteemed him, if that's a word, even as an artist, it appears. Too much show about him for their liking, and they saw through it. J. R. says they must have known that most of his anticking meant precisely nothing and threw no light whatever on the music; which in turn means very little to me.

From this you will have gathered that I saw Ransom to-night. But he kept me such an unconscionable time*—to good purpose, however—that I can't possibly send you our findings now. It must keep till to-morrow. At this moment the clock strikes

---

* I feel that Lorwood could never have resisted putting this into inverted commas and adding "as Charles II might have said."

midnight dramatically, as they would say in a novel, as though a clock could discriminate between one situation and another! But this must necessarily modify my preceding sentence. I now say, with greater truth, that I will send you the stuff to-day.

Au revoir (mais quand?)

ALAN.

COPY OF AILNER'S REPORT

(not edited!)

DET.-INSP. HOPE.

SIR,

I went to Harmsford-on-Sea, on Sat., Oct. 1st, as per instructions and am pleased to report some results re the late Sir Noel Grampian.

My investigations began with a visit to the Manager of the Harmsford-on-Sea Pavilion Orchestra, Mr. Hilbert, whom I duly interrogated, as instructed, taking particular note of the article on Sir Noel Grampian's past career published in the *Maningpool Telegraph*. I may mention that I learned from the gentleman in question that Lady Grampian is still living at Harmsford, but he felt that it would be useless as well as tactless for me to call on her, as she had not lived with her husband since he left and would not be likely to know anything useful, also that what she did know of events here she would doubtless not feel inclined to divulge. I decided not to interview Lady Grampian and not to bring pressure to bear on her unless all other sources of information failed, and it subsequently transpired that the desired information was forthcoming elsewhere. If it should prove insufficient, I felt that perhaps a higher authority could consult Lady Grampian to greater advantage later on, if necessary.

The other information obtained, however, proved interesting so far as it went. I began by asking who "those in authority" were who had been so impressed by Grampian's conducting and was told, a little scornfully I thought, that they were all authorities on municipal affairs, but by no means on music; in fact they were the Committee appointed to form the new orchestra, all of them members of the Municipal Council and not a professional musician among them. Some, however, the Manager said, prided themselves not a little on their love of music, and it was they who had carried a motion to form a real orchestra out of what had been only the small band usually found at seaside places.

As regards the action for breach of contract brought by the Thomas Hilkington Opera Co., Mr. Hilbert informed me that the *Maningpool Telegraph* took too much upon itself in suggesting that it was undeserved. As he put it, "if ever anyone deserved a good wigging, it was that bounder Grampian"; but I take it that he is not altogether unprejudiced either. It was quite clear, seemingly, that the Opera Co. would have had a case, as Grampian undoubtedly broke his contract in order to take up the Harmsford appointment, a matter about which he had cleverly left the Harmsford authorities in ignorance. To put it bluntly, he had told them an untruth and pretended that he was free to accept their contract. No action was brought against him, however, because Mr. Thos. Hilkington was thoughtless enough to say before witnesses that although he was entitled to damages, he would in fact be glad to be rid of the conductor, who had made himself objectionable and caused endless trouble by undesirable conduct. Grampian was thereupon advised to threaten a counter-action for slander and the Opera Co. being already in low water and unwilling to risk having to pay legal costs, abandoned proceedings.

On asking for particulars of the "undesirable conduct," I was told that nothing definite was known and that it may all have been an invention of Mr. Hilkington; but it was rumoured that Grampian had been "unprofessional" in his attitude to some of the ladies of the company, especially among the chorus. Mr. Hilbert told me, as a purely personal view, that he had heard of Grampian making love to several of these girls at once, and that instead of keeping the matter to themselves, they told each other and so became suspicious or jealous, or perhaps frightened. In Mr. Hilbert's opinion Grampian would have had more success if he had confined his attentions to one at a time; but against this it must be observed that he is a rather cynical man and, having been associated with Grampian as Manager, has very little, if anything, to say in favour of that gentleman.

Nevertheless, subsequent evidence showed that this was certainly a case of strong philandering inclinations, to put it no higher. On inquiring as to the quarrel with the Municipality mentioned by the *Maningpool Telegraph*, I heard that same was due to a cheese-paring policy pursued by a majority of the Committee that became ever stronger during the eleven years of the conductor's activities at Harmsford. As to the opposition of one particular member, it appears that it did not lead to Grampian's resignation, but was the direct cause of his dismissal. The Harmsford Council, I was told, did not greatly mind him announcing to the world that he was leaving of his own accord, so long as he went, and the member in question in fact preferred that it should be so, for personal reasons of his own.

This brings me to my subsequent interview with Councillor Rossingham, to whom Mr. Hilbert recommended me to apply for further particulars, as he was acquainted with the exact nature of the personal quarrel, though he hinted that he could tell things if he chose. I found Councillor Rossingham very reserved indeed at first and most reluctant to discuss the matter in question. It was necessary for me to make strong representations to him about the gravity of withholding information from the Police in a case of murder, and only after assuring him that he need not necessarily mention the names of people who might be involved could I elicit some particulars.

It transpired that Grampian had by no means relinquished the flirtatious habits he had cultivated when with the Opera Co. and that there had been various little scandals connected with his name at Harmsford, although nothing of the kind occurred until some two or three years after his marriage to Miss Laetitia Parkings, a young Harmsford lady, in 1922. Matters came to a head, after some small troubles of the kind, when the daughter of a friend and colleague of Mr. Rossingham began to spend weekends in London under the pretext of staying there with a former school-friend of hers. Mrs. Grampian (as she then was), whose suspicions were aroused by repeated absences of her husband "on business" (and it is true that he often managed to combine his trips to town with broadcasting engagements), began to make enquiries, subsequently communicating her doubts to the family of Mr. Rossingham's friend, whereupon the intrigue, if indeed it was such,* was discovered. Mr. Rossingham then took it upon himself, in order to avoid exposing his friend's family, to make representations of this state of affairs to the Orchestra Committee, and he himself moved at a meeting that Grampian should be dismissed his post as soon as possible, a motion that was unanimously carried.

The only further piece of information I was able to elicit, also from Councillor Rossingham, was that Lady Grampian (as she now is) refused to live with her husband after this incident, at which he inconsiderately expressed his intense relief, whereupon she, in order to annoy him in turn, declared that she would never consent to divorce him, should he at any time require her to do so. She thereafter returned to her parents, whose home is still at Harmsford, and it is quite true, as the *Maningpool Telegraph* observes, that she has never set foot in Maningpool since her husband's appointment there, although her sister's house, situated in that city, had previously been almost a second home to her.

(SIGNED) W. J. AILNER.

---

* Chivalrous Ailner! But indeed and indeed, I do think it must have been "such."

Thursday, 6th October

DEAR, PATIENT JULIA,

Here now is Ransom's report, as I suppose I *may* call this document. (According to that ass Lorwood, Ransom loathes it if anybody calls one of his criticisms a "report." Their mutual contempt is most entertaining when you get them separately and must be even more so when they are together, doubtless as sportingly amiable as two rivals in front of their lady-love.) As I told you, it was nearly midnight when I got back to the pub, and I spent some time copying that list of the orchestra he made for me, with signs against the players who in his opinion could have done the deed. Here it is, together with Ransom's professional observations and some comments added by me. What do you make of it all?

Impossible to write more this morning. Frantically busy. Letters have begun to come in from the orch. Oh Lord! Am I to ignore most of them on the strength of J. R.'s speculations? It looks like it, but I daren't. They've got not only to be read, but to be followed up, I fear.

Thine for aye,

ALAN.

I'll send the orch. letters as I can spare them or get them copied. They must be in the *dossier.*—Oh yes, J. R. looks the part. Bearded, but not too fiercely, and he wears a braided velvet jacket in the house. Picturesque. Not sure yet if he isn't a humbug. Talks sense about his job—to me, if that's anything. I asked him for other cuttings of his stuff about N. G., by the way; he'll send them, and I'll pass them on to you, or duplicates if I need them.

Jasper Ransom's Statement

Wednesday, 5th October

I have already outlined my reasons for supposing that the shot was fired simultaneously with the cymbal clash at cue number 79 in my article in last Monday's *Maningpool Telegraph*. With these reasons I now find that Detective-Inspector Hope is inclined to agree.

My aim now is to show Mr. Hope, whom I am asking to corroborate my statements at every point, that the full score shows conclusively that only a few of the players could possibly have fired the shot, always assuming that it really was fired at that point. (The medical evidence, Mr. Hope tells me, is perfectly consistent with that view, and my own reasoning in my "Musical Notes" convinces him that I am right in saying that the shot would have been heard anywhere in the neighbourhood of that cymbal clash, except if fired simultaneously with that clash itself.)

We will now draw up a list of all the players concerned in "Ein

Heldenleben"; in other words, a list of those who appear in the first place to be suspects. It is as follows:

    m   1 Piccolo
        3 Flutes
        3 Oboes   ⎫
                   ⎬ 4 Oboes
        1 Cor anglais ⎭
        1 Eb Clarinet
        2 Clarinets (ordinary)
        1 Bass Clarinet
        3 Bassoons
        1 Double Bassoon
        8 Horns
        5 Trumpets
        3 Trombones
        1 Tenor Tuba
        1 Bass Tuba
    m   2 Harps
        1 Solo Violin
        12 Violins I (including solo)
        10 Violins II
        8 Violas
        8 Cellos
        6 Double Basses
    m   Kettle-Drums (1st percussion player)
    m   Small Side Drum (2nd do.)
    m   Snare Drum or Tenor Drum (3rd do.)
        Cymbals (4th do.)
    m   Bass Drum (5th do.)

We now have to see which of these players were busy at the given passage and which not, and reference to the full score makes this perfectly clear. On the face of it those not engaged at the moment, who could therefore have fired the shot, are only the piccolo, the two harps, the kettle-drums, and all the other drums. We will therefore mark those on the list above with an *m* (for murder), this being only for our private eyes. All the others are out of the question, *according to the score*. But, as I point out to Mr. Hope, there are certain qualifications to be made, some in favour of, others against, certain players. On that basis I should be inclined to rule out the harpists and the first percussionist, and to suspect, on the other hand, more or less any of the strings, except perhaps the first and second violins seated in the front row facing the stalls.

These violinists are exonerated simply by reason of their very conspicuous positions, as will be seen from the sketch-plan of the orchestral seating Mr. Hope has thoughtfully procured from the Orchestra's Secretary. It is inconceivable, we both agree, that any player so plainly visible from all parts of the hall could have dared to level a murderous weapon at the conductor even for a second or two.

The harps, we feel, are also ruled out by a question of position, if not by the fact that they are women, one of them, Miss Jarvis, a rather timid slip of a girl, the other the wife of Prof. Gillighan, a lady of a certain social position, and moreover the deceased's sister-in-law. (This latter point, however, calls for a query, we are inclined to think.)

The timpanist is pretty safe from serious suspicion on purely musical grounds, as Mr. Hope could not be expected to see, and indeed many musicians would doubtless overlook. He was idle, it is true, at the moment the shot was fired (according to our hypothesis), but he had been busy only fifteen bars before and was going to be busy again only four bars later. Not only that, but—and this is my chief point, visible only to a specialist—his three kettle-drums

were tuned to E♭, B♭, and A♭ just before the shot, whereas immediately afterwards two of them would have had to play B♮ and F♯.
This means that two of his three drums had to be re-tuned during
a mere nineteen bars of fairly quick time, and that he therefore had
quite as much to do as any of those who actually played.

The conclusion to which one must inevitably come, then, is
that the chief suspect—to put it no more strongly—is the piccolo.

Alan Hope's Postscript

That is, indeed, the conclusion on musical grounds; but some of
Mr. Ransom's points seem to be as insufficient as in some ways,
I agree with him, they will probably turn out to be essential. I
grant, for the moment, that we may rule out the harps and the
kettle-drums, for reasons already shown, and that any of the
strings except those in the front row are under suspicion. As for
the other percussionists, apart from the kettle-drummer (or must
I call him "timpanist"?), who is anyhow above suspicion, it would
be almost a miracle if they were guilty, for they were placed too
high up on the platform to have fired the shot at the angle at
which it was found in the body. N. G. would have had to indulge
his habit of leaning back (if that was one of his habits) too peril-
ously for the bullet to pass into him almost horizontally.

But this leaves me with nobody but the piccolo, and I should
hesitate a long time before I made him my only suspect, even if
I knew he had a motive, which at the moment I do not. And if
he did have a motive, so had a number of others, I have very little doubt. Grampian's relations with the players in his orchestra
must have been very much the same all round. I cannot imagine

that the relationship was a personal one anywhere, always excepting Beatrice, of course.

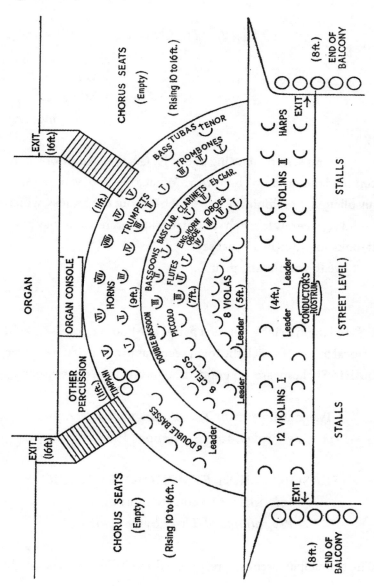

Friday, 7th October

M'POOL.

Friday morning.

D. J.,

Ransom sent the cutting about N. G.'s first symphony concert held this autumn (herewith). What a squirt of venom. Also,
unsolicited, a preliminary screed of his about the Strauss, which
I send you merely for such special musical interest as it may have.
It looks sound to me. What say?

Love to you and the infants,

ALAN.

P.S. Tell them to look out for a parcel of M'pool Lumps—a kind
of local toffee of which the town seems as proud as if it had given
birth to Shakespeare. It's good, though, and won't upset them.

Two cuttings from *The Maningpool Telegraph*
Friday, 16th September 1938

SEASON'S FIRST SYMPHONY CONCERT
SIR NOEL GRAMPIAN'S RETURN
Programme of Three Symphonies

The Municipal Orchestra reappeared at the Civic Hall last night before a large assembly that was ready to welcome a new series of Symphony Concerts with much warmth and a certain amount of curiosity, justified by a not unadventurous season's programme. The public was also disposed to give a rousing reception to Sir Noel Grampian, who is in charge of Maningpool's orchestral music for the fourth season running. There was the sort of uproar it gives an audience peculiar pleasure to indulge in to the top of its bent, and which Sir Noel himself shows no signs of disliking.

Be that as it may, however; it is yesterday's music that matters, whatever people who care more for social than for artistic events may say. Let us, therefore, proceed to its discussion. The programme, though conventional and not too well balanced, consisted simply of three Symphonies: Mozart's in G minor, Schubert's "Unfinished" and, in the second part, Tchaikovsky's No. 5. No overture or other short piece preceded this scheme as a concession to the usual stragglers who cannot forsake their dinner (or high tea) tables (or is it their dressing-tables?) in good time; but in order that we should not miss the usual noisy and unperturbable display of bad manners, the doors were opened after the first movement of Mozart, and the pleasure of the more civilised, punctual, and scrupulous members of the audience was utterly spoilt by a barbarous invasion.

It will have been gathered by the perspicacious reader, even if he was not there to notice it, that the programme was so chosen as to include no solo performer. Sir Noel Grampian was, in fact, his own star, and indeed he twinkled with a will all through the evening. (Need it be said that the present writer intends no malicious reference to the "little star" of the nursery rhyme, his bosom being, as everyone knows by this time, wholly innocent of suchlike heinous offences?) Sir Noel literally threw himself into his task in his usual impetuous manner—a manner unfortunately much better suited to secondary than to great music. If it thus amounts to a disparagement to say that his Tchaikovsky was in its way magnificent while his Mozart and Schubert were only so-so, that is to be regretted, but cannot be helped. It is the simple truth that the G minor Symphony sounded on the whole strident and hectoring—the slow movement being, for compensation, made almost degradingly sentimental—and that the "Unfinished" at once got itself into a distressing state of unhealthy excitement from which it never recovered, not even in the most serene moments of the *Andante con moto*. There could be no profit in discussing such performances in detail. For the moment they are best suffered in silence, though there is no telling that the time will not come—and come soon, if we cannot have great music treated more musically—when the full fury of critical exasperation will break over Sir Noel's head. Meanwhile, let us be like Patience on a monument—in this particular case a monument erected to the memory of two mangled masterpieces.

As for the Tchaikovsky performance, it hit us all where we live. There is no gainsaying the immense effectiveness of Sir Noel's methods in music so self-centred and exhibitionist as the Fifth Symphony, and one does not deny him a certain virtuosity in conducting any more than one denies a certain virtuosity in flying to a sea-gull. But even here one is bound to say that there is at once more and less in the work than he succeeds in bringing out. There is more sheer music and less hysteria. Still, as a piece of ranting theatricality the performance was magnificent, and the only question is whether those who showed a quite immoderate—indeed almost immodest—admiration of Sir Noel's treatment of Tchaikovsky are right in being quite so willing to sacrifice Mozart and Schubert to such a frenzied orgy as we were treated to last night. Well, there is no disputing about taste, as my esteemed colleague of the *Messenger* would no doubt say in the original Latin. It is all a question of whether one would rather see Sardou played by a Sarah Bernhardt or Shakespeare by the often no more than moderate talents of Stratford-on-Avon.

All the same, there is a peculiar danger about such playing as Tchaikovsky received last night. (It was very decent, so far as the orchestra was concerned, and an early opportunity shall be taken of discussing its present quite adequate constitution and capacities further.) This danger is that such conducting as Sir Noel's makes it almost superfluous to listen to music at all. His antics on the rostrum, which have certainly lost none of their extravagance since last season, are so graphically revealing of what the composer intends, that very soon the public will no longer come to a concert to *hear* the message of a symphony, but merely to *see* it as interpreted by the conductor's actions. The time will come when we shall be asking that Sir Noel should be compelled by the Orchestra's Committee to conduct behind a screen, lest he should corrupt our listeners into spectators. In any case, it is becoming positively dangerous for all but those with the strongest hearts, and perhaps the most susceptible ones, to watch him at his work. His violent striding from side to side of the rostrum to its very edge, his precipitate leaps and collapses, and his giddy lurchings backwards and forwards are becoming too much of a good thing—if indeed they have ever been that at all.

J. R.

Monday, 26th September 1938

MUSICAL NOTES

STRAUSS'S "HELDENLEBEN"

It appears that there has been some disagreement among the members of the Municipal Orchestra's Committee as to the desirability of performing Richard Strauss's symphonic poem, "Ein Heldenleben," at the season's second Symphony Concert next Thursday. I understand that Sir Noel Grampian, at a rather stormy Committee meeting, had to go to unprecedented lengths of plain speaking, coupled with veiled threats of resignation, before even a slight majority of votes was to be gained in favour of what one of the more classically-minded members picturesquely described as "this feast of Trimalchian extravagance."

Now I am far from wishing to suggest that a performance of "A Hero's Life" will fulfil one of my heart's more ardent desires, and it is possible that readers will have gathered before now that I could probably survive Sir Noel's withdrawal from our musical scene; but there can be no doubt that the Maningpool public is entitled to such experiences and since the City has never before heard this work, which is after all a remarkable and representative one, it is about time that it were produced, forty years after its composition, which was finished in December, 1898.

Our orchestra is kept going with funds derived from the

proceeds of its concerts and from the rates—in other words, by the public's money, and it seems too high-handed for the Committee to try to prohibit a performance merely because it is expensive. There is no moral objection—at any rate of a kind discernible by a body of estimable citizens who are not musicians and for the most part not even musically cultivated laymen—to this work by Strauss, and failing that, one does not see why the Symphony Concert audiences should not be given a taste of it, even if it proves to be unpalatable to a majority of hearers.

If only on principle, I am glad that the performance is to take place on Thursday. Anything else would have been as intolerable to myself as to Sir Noel, if he can bear the idea of my seeing eye to eye with him for once in a way. That I have any great liking for Strauss in general, or for this symphonic poem in particular, would be too much to pretend, though I recognise the immense skill that went to its making. Its general scheme, which is that of a megalomaniac's autobiography, does not commend it to one's affection, and the musical material is, as usual with Strauss, a mixture of good, not so good and downright bad, blended without the least evidence that the composer had any notion of the difference. That the music is often displeasing is not due, as one hopes even the most reactionary of Maningpool's concert-goers will understand, to its being "modern," for it is that no longer after forty years, though a great to-do was made about its alleged audacity when it was new. If such a feature as the unbearably protracted "Battle" episode remains offensive, it is simply because it never was good music, and never will be. It is, so to speak, sub-musical.

Even the orchestration, which is in its way masterly and immensely effective, has its serious faults, the chief of which is

Strauss's inveterate habit of doubling his parts, often many times over, so that one rarely hears the tone of any instrument alone, but gets everything conveyed to the ear in a thick paste of indeterminate sound. It is a kind of safety-scoring, one may say, for it would be quite possible for all sorts of instruments to drop out of the performance for a minute or two without anybody missing them, if he judged by the ear alone. That is why only the other day, at a rehearsal of "A Hero's Life" I attended—it was before Sir Noel so courteously cut me off the visiting-list—it was quite easy to allow the fourth oboist to relinquish his part without the least damage to the music some time before he came to the break where he changes over to the cor anglais, in order to save his breath for a part that stands out prominently in the latter instrument.

It is here, in this endless duplicating of similar parts, that Strauss is so extravagant, and if the Orchestra's Committee had had the knowledge to object to "A Hero's Life" on technical grounds, they might have had a leg to stand on when they nearly voted next Thursday's performance out of existence. As it was, they had not even a crutch, and we have no patience with mere niggardliness. Let us therefore congratulate ourselves that Maningpool is to have this performance, whatever may be thought of the work in question.

J. R.

FOUR GEORGES HOTEL,
MANINGPOOL.

7. X. 38.

DARLING,

I just dashed off that note this morning, with J. R.'s cuttings, but didn't say I was going to the Gillighans to tea, at my own invitation. The first few letters from the orch. members show that something rankled seriously among them, and I wanted to know more about that deputation to Humphrey. Sure enough, there was any amount of unrest. I jotted down what I thought of interest, and I daresay more will transpire when other letters arrive.

Briefly, this is what happened. On September 14, the day before the first symphony concert of the season, Humphrey, as Chairman of the orchestra, was visited in solemn state by thirteen members who, it appears, hold what may be called the key-positions in the band. They were the leader, Eltham, the four principals of the other string groups you will find on the orchestra list I sent you, Beckenham (1st flute), Simmons (1st oboe), Evans (1st clarinet), Tufton (1st bassoon), Stillingham (1st horn), Holborne (1st trumpet), Mere (1st trombone) and Dipton (timpanist: Humphrey says it must not be spelt tympanist). All in high dudgeon, it appears, or at any rate dudgeons of various degrees of elevation—a state, by the way, which I had already diagnosed from some of the letters from the orch.

Humphrey says there were no very definite accusations, but it all boils down to the fact that the whole band, if we may take the deputation to have been representative of it, regarded N. G. artistically speaking as a humbug and personally as a cad and a bully. In fact, I repeat, as N. B. G.! They had assembled only a couple of days earlier—on the 12th, I see from my notes—but after the first three rehearsals (of a familiar programme deliberately chosen to start the season with because it did not call for very much preparation) they'd had pretty well enough of him. He'd got much worse than ever before, they declared, and they vowed that they could not see how they could possibly face another whole season under him. Was there, the long and the short of it was, no way of getting rid of him then and there? Of course Humphrey was bound to point out, though he secretly sympathised with them, as well he might where his precious brother-in-law is concerned, that a contract was a contract, that the city fathers could hardly be expected to pay up for a breach thereof, and that unless N. B. G. himself committed such a breach, there was nothing to be done, at any rate for this year. Whether, indeed, anything could be done for the next three was doubtful, as the agreement had been renewed until the end of the season of 1940–41. Apparently there were some veiled allusions to a possible strike on the part of the orchestra, but Humphrey pointed out how unwise anything of the kind would be, as N. G. had the power to dismiss any player at three months' notice and would doubtless not hesitate to take steps to get rid of anyone whom he considered directly responsible for the revolt, in other words the leading members, meaning of course the deputation, whereupon Holborne, who is under notice already, spoke up hotly and said it didn't seem to make any difference anyhow, and that during the very first three rehearsals three members had been dismissed, and would have been fired on the spot but for the three months' notice clause in their agreement, which was a disgraceful injustice if it did not equally apply to the conductor. Dashwood, the first viola, who is a hot-tempered, impatient sort of chap, Humphrey tells me, then said that although he held no brief for N. G., goodness knew, it was jolly well some of the chaps' own fault if they were fired. And it appears that one of the other two is Gough, the third viola, who got the sack for alleged incompetence and insubordination. And who do you think the third is?

No other than Repton, who plays either third flute or, as the case may be, piccolo. Observe, my love. Who did Ransom say was the chief suspect? Observe and reflect, to be sure, but at the same time don't make a vast deal of this.

It's this man Dashwood who still interests me very much, in spite of the fact that I think the suggestion of the revolver's lying bang in front of him too crude for anything. Somehow I can't persuade myself to dissociate him from the case altogether. Humphrey says he *is* an interesting chap, desperately keen on his work and a fine teacher of the violin and viola, which he professes at the local Institute of Music, at Humphrey's recommendation, in fact. A bit of a bore, though, apparently; one of those terribly earnest people who must always show how keen they are. Always asking "interesting" questions or making "clever" suggestions. It appears that he drove N. G. nearly to distraction the first two seasons, much to Humphrey's secret delight, by continually showing off at rehearsals in that way and conveying, somehow, how different he was from the rest of the orchestral herd, how understanding and sensitive and what not. N. G. could stand it no longer eventually and snubbed him disgustingly all through the third season, in front of everybody.

He can't leave Humphrey alone either. Even at that meeting he had to show off by asking H. whether he could lend him the score of "Heldenleben" for a day or two. He could have got it from the Public Library, H. says, but that would have been so much less impressive. Not that H.'s collection is to be sniffed at, and he is always ready, Beatrice says, to let others have the benefit of it. You should see his study and the adjacent library! So upstairs he went and got that score for D.—that famous score even I ought to know by now. And then, of course, D. had to make a number of interesting points then and there, asking the Prof. questions, but really telling him all the time. He appears to be insufferable, and I am beginning to feel he *ought* to have murdered N. G. But he's obviously no fool. I wonder what his letter to me will be like.

How will that do for one day? Darling, I begin to feel that I have no right to inflict these screeds on you. If all this business makes you feel as I do at the moment—pursuing but faint—I think I ought to desist. Only it does seem to sift things putting them down like that, all in a heap, and then getting rid of all the entangling rubbish, keeping only a few notes of each day's salient points in a note-book that partakes of both a calendar and a chart. Bless you for your help, which would be enough if you merely accepted these outpourings, though your suggestions are always helpful, whether they lead to anything or not.

Eternally your own,

ALAN.

P.S. I refuse to take any notice of your would-be shrewd guess (and no doubt you don't want me to, since Ailner's document was sent to you so horribly confidentially) that the lady in question was the sage Mr. Rossingham's own daughter. Beware! Shall I have to turn Petruchio and indulge in a little taming of the shrewd?

Saturday, 8th October

4 G.S,
M'POOL.

8. X. 38.

DARLING JULIA,

Yes, you *were* clever. I couldn't trust myself to say so, but Ransom acknowledges it, and *he* knows. I submitted your suggestion to him and he was ready to kick himself for not seeing the implication of his own criticism of Strauss's scoring. Of course he saw at once that you're right: he did say in his article of Sept. 26 that so many parts were doubled in the score of "Heldenleben" that any number of players might drop out for a moment without its being noticed. Good Lord! What then becomes of his suggestion that only a few people could have done it? Now it seems that almost anyone could. At a pinch *absolutely* anybody but the cymbal player. So where are we?

Here is a list drawn up with R.'s help, showing by various signs how things now stand. Study, ponder and digest it, my pet. My head reels. What now, eh?

Yours distractedly,

ALAN.

			Revised List of Suspects
s	p	i	1 Piccolo
s	p	e	3 Flutes
p	e		4 Oboes (Cor anglais playing 4th)
s	p	e	1 E♭ Clarinet
s	p	e	2 Clarinets
s	p	e	1 Bass Clarinet
p	e		3 Bassoons
s	p	e	1 Double Bassoon
d	e		8 Horns
d	e		5 Trumpets
d	e		3 Trombones
d	e		1 Tenor Tuba
d	e		1 Bass Tuba
o	i		2 Harps
d	e		6 Violins I (including solo)
p	e		6 Violins I
d	e		5 Violins II
p	e		5 Violins II
p	e		8 Violas
s	p	e	8 Cellos
d	e		6 Double Basses
o	e		Kettle-Drums
d	i		Small Side Drum
d	i		Snare Drum or Tenor Drum
o	e		Cymbals
d	i		Bass Drum

If we bear in mind Mrs. Hope's just observation that, supposing
J. R. is right in saying that many players might momentarily drop

out of the performance of Strauss undetected, then according to the score of "Heldenleben" almost any member of the orchestra might have shot N. G. The list of possible suspects is thus once again enormously enlarged. Not quite so enormously, however, as would appear from a glance at pages 152–3 of the score, which would seem to show that, so far as dropping out goes, almost anybody but the cymbal player could have fired, nobody being for the moment absolutely essential to the sound. There are no solo leads here and all the parts are doubled over and over again, except the repeated chords in the trumpets and trombones, some notes of which, and especially the bass A♭, which is not supported elsewhere in the score, it would have been dangerous to omit. Actually there are only three separate parts going on apart from those brass chords: the high E♭ for flutes, E♭ clarinet and first violins, the fervent tune played in octaves by the four oboes, two B♭ clarinets, bass clarinet, the three bassoons, second violins and violas, and the sprawling principal theme rising high up from the bass and divided between the double bassoon, the horns (the low second, fourth, sixth and eighth playing the first phrases and the high first, third, fifth and seventh continuing with the second), tenor tuba, cellos and double basses. Nearly everybody is busy, and we have marked the performers actually engaged in playing, so far as the score can tell us, with an *e*. Those which happen to be idle, on the other hand, we have marked *i*. But we have been obliged to use another set of markings, showing not what the score tells us, but what J. R.'s suggestion about ceasing to play against the composer's instructions implies. We have given up our *m* for "murder," such a hypothesis having for the moment become untenable, and are now marking some of the players with a *p* for possible murderers, others with a *d* for doubtful ones, and a few (only four, unfortunately) with an *o* for being out of the question. Even that small number may be reduced if one cannot agree that the kettle-drummer was too busy re-tuning two of his instruments to have got in a shot, and we may also have to bear in mind that if he knew he was going to kill N. G. and that the performance was going to stop, he need not have re-tuned at all, though that might, if discovered, have exposed him to instant detection; but he is at least very doubtful, like the rest of the players seated on the top range of the orchestral platform, which is almost certainly at the wrong angle for the shot. In other words, if he were not eligible for *o*, he would certainly be for *d*. We have marked all the players at the top *d* for another reason that has already been shown as almost conclusive proof against the murderer's being seated so high up and so far away: the revolver could almost certainly not have been flung into the well in front of the viola leader from so far off.

On analysing the above we find that the only player who is marked "possible" *and* "idle" is the piccolo. He was moreover seated in a straight line opposite the conductor and just above the spot where the pistol was found; all of which makes him, purely theoretically, our chief suspect for the moment. Let us therefore give him an additional mark of *s*. But that is hardly fair if we can possibly find others who may look particularly suspicious according to some special theoretical point; and here again we must consult the score. We have no reason to change our view that the shot was most probably fired on the cymbal clash at cue number 79, and although we have learnt to distrust the evidence of the score, we have no right to ignore its indications altogether.

Among these indications we see, for instance, that the two B♭ clarinets and the bass clarinet have three bars' rest before figure 79 and half a bar's after—hardly enough time to level and fire a gun if the music is actually played as written, but enough to justify our giving these players an *s* too. The cellos also have the three bars' rest, but come in on the first beat at 79. Still, one of them might have failed to enter, so that they too receive an *s*. The double bassoon and bass tuba both leave off playing one bar after 79 and do not resume for some pages, and the flutes leave off for a moment two bars after 79, and one of them might have dropped out earlier, since they play nothing more conspicuous than a high sustained E♭ in unison. The same is true of the E♭ clarinet. If we assume that the shot could have been fired unheard *after* the cymbal clash, any of these people come under suspicion, except the tuba player, who is ruled out by his position in the orchestra. We therefore give an *s* also to the flutes, the E♭ clarinet and the double bassoon.

J. R. AND A. H.

Sunday, 9th October

Dearest,

It only just occurs to me that you will get a fearful budget to-morrow morning, as I posted you a Shavian preface yesterday, and of course you'll get it together with the enclosed first batch of letters from the orchestra. I am not sending them all; some are mere biographical précis and others the baldest statements of no significance and arousing no possible suspicion, especially in conjunction with the eliminations Ransom and I have attempted. But some may amuse, touch, interest or disquiet you, each after its kind. Here they are.

I am myself uneasy about one or two. I have asked Mr. Gough, for instance, to grant me an interview to-morrow—at the Orchestra's office—for his letter is altogether a little too detached for my liking. I want to ask him why it has not occurred to him that he need not leave at all, now that the man who sacked him is no more. Is it natural that he should not have thought of that?

Beatrice insisted in her charmingly unyielding way that I should lunch out at Rookdale again. Well, I didn't mind. It was a delightfully Indian-summerish sort of day and the old gardens and brick walls and trees of that pleasant suburb were perfectly matched by the weather, and that again by the Gillighans' always inviting table, a nice change from the square-cut excellence of the bill of fare (one could not possibly call it a menu there) of the 4 G.s. I'm sure Rookdale, being very much aware of its dignity, is the standing joke of all the Maningpool pantomimes at Christmas— and I shall probably see them, as my case shows so few signs of moving—but it is none the worse for that. Even the tram ride from here is pleasant on such a day. You first walk down the crooked and rather narrow but really distinguished Saltergate— M'pool's Bond Street, with its old-fashioned confectioner's shop (Pollock's, where I get the children's M'pool Lumps, and which is one of the six or seven "original" M. L. shops in the town!), the most real thing in apothecaries (not chemists) I have ever seen, its arty-and-crafty depot for Galpin's pottery, its smart modern Jaeger branch, its Tudoresque W. H. Smith, and so on. Then you board (why board?) one of those narrow, *affairés*, cream and pale-blue trams, and off you go through one or two streets of what they call the "city" here: and they look it, especially on a Sunday morning, when they are absolutely dead and deserted. From the top of the tram you see all the first-floor type-writing, solicitors', accountants' and other offices, pass the art gallery, a Florentine palazzo as black as and much sootier than your hat; then round the corner into the pleasant Bluecoat Square, with its green patch and rapidly sereing plane-trees in the middle. After that, another twist, and up the mild incline of Tipworth Avenue, rather like Milsom Street at Bath, only much longer, much more callow, though with some handsome Nash-cum-Cheltenham houses and shops, all very airy and pleasing in a provincially snobbish sort of way—the kind of provincial street, all the same, that looks much more like that of a Continental capital than anything in

London you can think of. Then, at the top, the tram gently and suddenly lowers itself to level ground, like a duck into water, and stops at a natty modern iron and glass shelter in a geometrical array of little grass plots surrounded by borders of overlapping hoops about the height of a *dachshund*, but quite incapable of keeping any other kind of *hund* off the lawn. However, everybody at Rookdale behaves perfectly. Two stops after that along a main road bordered mostly by low stuccoed terraces with pretty pillared and pedimented doorways, separated from the pavement by trim privet hedges and broad driveways, you "alight"—since you must do something corresponding to "boarding" and sufficiently genteel for Rookdale—you alight, say I, where Oakwood Avenue, the Gillighans' road, and Acacia Drive, the late lamented N. G.'s, meet you at right angles on either side. And so into the hospitable arms of Beatrice and Humphrey. You will wonder why I didn't stay with them; it all sounds so nice, and is. Well, perhaps that's the very reason. Or possibly the fact that Beatrice declared that you *can't* stay at the Four Georges. Oh, can't I? What's more, though tell it not in Rookdale, I *like* staying at the Four Georges.

Forgive me: this was going to be a note, and here I go again. But at least it's a change from shop and thus nice for me, if not for you.

So would you and the kids be. But oh! when shall I be done here? Shall I have to ask you all to join me and take you to those pantomimes?

Much love to the lot of you,

Ever yours,

ALAN.

37 FRAMPTON ROAD,
ROOKDALE,
MANINGPOOL.

7. OCT. 1938

DEAR SIR,

As Leader of the Maningpool Orchestra—a position I have occupied since its inception, not only because of such competence as I may flatter myself to possess, but also, perhaps, because I have been a resident musician of some reputation for a good many years now—I feel it to be incumbent on me to answer your questions (or rather to anticipate questions which you have not yet put to me) as carefully as possible.

Under the circumstances, and because I think it quite likely that I may have a good deal to say, especially if you should care to cross-question me, would it not be better if I called on you, at your convenience and at any place you may care to appoint, in order to be at your full disposal? I shall be very glad indeed to do so and, if you do not mind my saying it, to make the personal acquaintance of one with whose distinguished services to the Country I am by no means unacquainted.

I may add that I fully realise how impossible it would be for you to grant a personal interview to every member of the Orchestra, or possibly I should say "any"; but we both hold responsible positions, and I hope I am not presumptuous if I feel that you may care to make an exception in my case. At any rate I hold myself fully at your disposal.

Believe me,

Very truly yours,
CONSTANT ELTHAM.

TRILBY COTTAGE,
GRAFTON-ON-THE-WATER,
NR. MANINGPOOL.

Oct. 6th, 1938.

DEAR SIR,

I beg to state that I am unable to account for the murder of Sir Noel Grampian in any way. I was busy playing when it occurred and as I did not happen to look at the conductor at that moment, when the tempo is quite firm and straightforward, I did not realise anything until I saw Sir Noel fall forward.

My engagement as first bassoon with the Maningpool Orchestra dates from the beginning of the season of 1935. I came here at the same time as Sir Noel, with whom I had been at Harmsford, where however I left only that season, and therefore was there for four years after he left. I came on his recommendation, as he seemed to have liked my work and remembered me after his tour abroad. I was a little doubtful about wanting to play under him again, but accepted on account of the favourable terms.

I remain, Dear Sir,
Yours faithfully,
DAVID M. TUFTON.

48, ASHLINGTON ROAD,
MANINGPOOL, 6.

8th October, 1938.

DEAR SIR,

At your request, I have pleasure in sending you the partic's you require. I assure you that I had no reason to dislike Sir Noel

Grampian, as I came here in the Autumn, 1935, at his own wish, as he had always considered me one of the best tympanists he had ever come across. You will excuse me saying so, but it is what Sir Noel told me himself, and I am anxious you should not think I had any grudge against him. I had played under him at Harmsford-on-Sea all the time he was there, and was there both before and after him.

Yours very sincerely,

F. S. DIPTON.

66, BLENHEIM DRIVE,

MANINGPOOL, 14.

October 7th, 1938.

DEAR SIR,

In accordance with your request I am writing down a few particulars about myself. I have been playing viola in the Maningpool Municipal Orchestra ever since 1929, and I was appointed principal of that section in 1934. I was given a Public School education, but unfortunately could not proceed to Oxford owing to a serious reverse in my father's fortunes.

But these details can be of no value to you, and I will therefore proceed to outline my ideas concerning the death of Sir Noel Grampian. I do not know whether the fact that the revolver was found lying in front of me has brought me under any serious suspicion in your mind, but I am fortunately blessed with sufficient imagination to realise that an investigator of your standing and, if I may say so, of your fame, could hardly proceed on so elementary an assumption. I can only assert with all the emphasis of which I am capable that I had nothing to do with the case, and that I am wholly at a loss to explain to myself how the revolver could have come to lie where it was. What is more, I place implicit trust in your powers of deduction, and do not for a moment suppose that I have anything to fear. I repeat, I am innocent.

Again bearing in mind your reputation for more than ordinary subtlety, I feel I can do myself no harm by referring quite frankly to the fact that I was by no means on pleasant terms with the late conductor. On the contrary, I am convinced that such frankness can only impress you in my favour. I am afraid Sir Noel was not a man capable of making himself liked by an orchestra; indeed he often seemed deliberately to go out of his way to court dislike, not to say detestation. I cannot well speak for other members of the orchestra, with whom I have very little to do, finding them, with few exceptions, far from congenial and rarely disposed to take any real interest in music or any other subject that matters.

Sir Noel's attitude towards me was cordial enough during his first two seasons here, and he was at least enough of a musician in a technical sense to be aware of the fact that I can play my instrument. He was even not disinclined at first to answer the questions relating to an orchestra's work which I felt it to be my duty to put to him occasionally, though my colleagues are far too much given to letting everything a conductor does or a composer demands pass unchallenged. Unfortunately at the end of the second season a serious quarrel broke out between us, due solely to Sir Noel's annoyance at having, quite unintentionally, exposed his ignorance of a musical term that is unusual enough, but occurs in an excessively familiar work every aspect of which a musician, and especially a conductor, may be expected to know. The point arose from Tchaikovsky's fifth Symphony, a work Sir

Noel must have been fond of, since he has done it twice in three seasons here, for we again had a shocking performance of it at the opening concert of the present season.

I do not know whether you are interested in music, but if you are, the matter will, I am sure, appeal to you as worthy of consideration. It concerns the slow movement, marked by the composer *Andante cantabile, con alcuna licenza,* which, as everybody with a smattering of Italian such as a musician ought to have knows as meaning "with *some* freedom." This, of course, was enough encouragement for Sir Noel to play Old Harry with the music in practically every bar, never taking two of them at the same speed, and this despite the fact that throughout the movement the frequent "licenses" indulged in by the composer are expressly indicated: *animando, sostenuto, con moto,* and so on. When I took the liberty at rehearsal to point this out to Sir Noel, he curtly dismissed my observation by saying that *alcuna licenza* meant "*every* freedom," a statement I was bound in sheer fairness to contradict, for where should we be if nobody ever tried to set mistakes right? We should live in an intellectual morass even worse than that in which our orchestra festers as it is. Finding himself defeated, Sir Noel then took the line of saying that, as the violas nowhere had anything of outstanding importance to play in this movement, the matter was no possible concern of mine; to which I could only retort, with some heat, I am afraid, that as nobody else ever had the pluck to dispute anything, I felt bound to take it upon myself, as I maintain I have a perfect right to do if I find that a composer's work is being deliberately distorted.

Sir Noel afterwards spoke to me in a manner that I can only describe as unpardonably insulting, and actually tried to make out that it was I who had been insolent, when I had been merely intellectually honest and, if I may say so, more courageous than any of my colleagues. He then took the usual line of the moral coward who knows himself in the wrong. He merely declined to enter into any further discussions with me, particularly in front of the whole orchestra (it was this that nettled him, I have no doubt), and he actually had the temerity to threaten me with dismissal for insubordination if I did not refrain from challenging him in this manner in future.

To this I was obliged to retort, first of all, that I would not mind submitting to anyone who could persuade me that he knew what he was talking about (or words to that effect), and secondly, that the Committee might have something to say to my dismissal, as I should certainly not hesitate to appeal to it and to state precisely what had led to our quarrel. That, I think, sufficiently intimidated him to make him refrain from acting upon his threat, for he knew perfectly well that he was in the wrong and that I might expose his appalling ignorance to the Committee, which has for its Chairman a musical scholar like Professor Gillighan, for whose learning I have the greatest respect. But he went so far as to urge the Committee to request me and, quite unnecessarily, the rest of the orchestra, not to enter into any dispute with the conductor in future— another most cowardly and despicable act. I need hardly add that we were not on speaking terms after that, and I resolutely declined to make any response to his feeble advances towards a reconciliation.

Please forgive me for having gone at such length into this unfortunate affair, but I felt that I had better put my cards on the table without delay. I need hardly add that I should be delighted to meet you, if you wish to discuss the case in greater detail.

Yours very truly,

THOMAS WILLOUGHBY DASHWOOD.

DETECTIVE-INSPECTOR ALAN HOPE,
FOUR GEORGES HOTEL,
MANINGPOOL.

c/o MRS. DIPSWORTH,
"HOLMEDENE,"
23, GRAFTON ROAD,
MANINGPOOL.

Oct. 6, 38.

DETECTIVE-INSPECTOR ALAN HOPE.

DEAR SIR,

Thank you very much for giving me the opportunity of writing to explain myself. I am glad to say that I am in a way quite out of touch with things here as yet, so I do not for a moment expect that you will think me capable of being concerned in this horrible affair, an experience which I am afraid I shall never forget. I have been in the orchestra here only from the beginning of this season, and Maningpool is not my home town. I have always lived with my parents at Teddington, so you see we both come from London. I am twenty-four and studied violin at the Royal Academy of Music, also the viola, which I now play in the orchestra here. I am afraid I knew very little indeed about Sir Noel, except what I heard from gossip, and that was not much, as I was so new and not well known to any of the other ladies in the orchestra. He spoke to me only once or twice, at the audition he gave me and once when I first came to a rehearsal, but he never deigned to address another word to me since. Perhaps I am not a *conspicuous* person, however.

Believe me,

Yours very truly,
Rosalind Lamb, L.R.A.M.

"The Dugout,"
Grafton-on-the-Water.

6. x. 38.

Dear Sir,

Just a brief note, to give you the desired information. I have been in the orchestra here since 1932, but had thought of giving notice at the end of this season, unless Sir Noel Grampian did so himself. I had the very worst possible opinion of him as a musician and doubted very much whether I should be able to endure another season under him, although I was bound by my agreement to do so until next Spring. As a man I did not like him, but then nobody did and I was not going to let that make any difference to me. If I could have respected him as a conductor, I should have been content to stay on. Unfortunately he was a charlatan and one of the worst conductors even this country has produced.

I pursued my musical studies at Leipzig, still the best possible place for a musical training, I consider, though it is now the fashion to say that home training is as good as any—a mistake, in my humble opinion. I doubt if I should have advanced to the post of leader of the second violins, if I had learnt to play as badly as some of the rank and file here. But then, I am something of a veteran, in fact, the second-oldest member of the Orchestra at present.

Yours truly,

FREDERICK D. GRANT.

8A WELLINGTON ROAD,
MANINGPOOL.
6th Oct., 1938.

DEAR SIR,

I hasten to accede to your request at once. There is very little I can say, I am afraid. The death of Sir Noel was a shock to me, I must say. Not personally, for I liked him as little as anybody else. But such a fright in the middle of a performance is too much for most people. I play first flute and sat almost straight in front of him. I saw it all, but I wish I had not done so. It was horrible.

I have been here ever since the Orchestra was started, but played second flute at first. Before long my talent was considered sufficient for me to advance to the post of principal. I am only twenty-nine. My studies were at the R.C.M. in London. I was supposed to go to Paris, because it was considered the best place for wind playing. But my father found he could not afford it, as through no fault of his own he lost money. I am not sorry now, as I consider our own country can give as good musical training as any other, if not better.

Believe me,

Yours sincerely,

ROBERT BECKENHAM.

RAWDON HOUSE,
FLAT 5,
MANINGPOOL, 3.

Oct. 6, 1938.

SIR,

You will receive so many letters that I had better make mine as brief as possible. I am sure you will have much unnecessary information to wade through. All I need say, I think, is that I have played double bass here since 1930, and I think Mr. Taplow, the Orchestra's Secretary, will vouch for my character, if you care to ask him. The late Sir Noel Grampian would have done so too, I am sure, if it were not for his unfortunate death, which I can only say I deplore. I am quite unable to throw any light on his murder.

Needless to say, I shall be pleased to answer any further questions you may like to ask.

Yours faithfully,

W. J. SPINNEY.

57, DILLING STREET,
BIRCHTON,
MANINGPOOL.

Oct. 7th, 1938.

DEAR SIR,

As you wish me to make a statement about the last Symphony Concert, I beg to say that I have been with the Municipal Orchestra since Sept., 1931. This was long before anybody thought of Sir Noel Grampian in this City and before several other members came who have been given precedence. I was born in 1903, if it is of any interest and before I came here I was in the orchestra at Billingborough in the summer and played at theatres in different towns during the winter.

I know nothing about the murder and have not thought about it, not being interested, as I am under notice to leave the Orchestra, having been dismissed by Sir Noel Grampian. There is enough to worry about without troubling myself about a matter that does not concern me in one way or the other. Not that I shall be down and out, as I can always go on playing violin at a music-hall here and shall not have to pay for a deputy on concert nights.

Yours faithfully,

R. B. GOUGH.

MUSICIANS' CLUB,
MANINGPOOL.

Oct. 8, 38.

DEAR SIR,

In answer to your demand, I should be only too pleased to help, but can at present think of nothing of any special interest. If you would care for me to call on you and have any questions to ask, shall be very pleased to do anything I can. Perhaps you will let me know. I am here most days and it reaches me quicker than at home. It is some way out, also there is a phone here (Allport 2976).

My instrument is second trumpet, since 1934 at M'pool.

Yours truly,

M. BEARDLING.

29, ALLPORT STREET,
MANINGPOOL, 4.

Oct. 8, 1938.

DEAR SIR,

Having received your request from Mr. Taplow, here are a few partic's re myself. I have been with the M'pool Orchestra since 1928, but played second Oboe before Sir Noel Grampian came, playing Cor Anglais as well when wanted, but he insisted on engaging another player so that works with 2 Ob's and C. A. could be played. I was offered to retain the 2nd Ob. but preferred the C. A., at a smaller salary, as I play Ob. at the M'pool Hippodrome and have to get a deputy when wanted by the Munic. Orch. So I only play there when a C. A. part or 3 Ob's is in the programme and otherwise at the Hippo.

I used to be at Music Halls before I joined the M'pool Orch.

Yrs. truly,

GEORGE LOVELOCK.

14, THE BUNGALOWS,
SHIFTON.

7th October, 1938.

DEAR SIR,

In answer to yours, I play first clarinet, was engaged as such in 1935.

I am unable to say what happened, much as I should like to help a Detective in distress, if you will excuse me. I can see your difficulty. The trouble is that I cannot remember in what position Sir Noel was just when the shot was fired. You see, he might have been turning any way, he was fairly spinning round sometimes.

As I always say to my colleagues, he doesn't conduct, he goes for walks, or used to, as I should say now. I am afraid you will have a very difficult case.

Believe me,

Sincerely yours,

B. EVANS.

MANINGPOOL, d. 6ten Okt.

DEAR MR. INSPEKTOR!

Forgive me, please, if I can tell you nothing about the so shocking murder of Sir Noel Grampian. I keep myself away from the Orchester so much as possible. I find that I can not have intelligent conversations about Music with nobody here. It is not possible: they think of nothing but to run away immediately after every Rehearsal, like work-men. They will not play for one minute more than they must and go so soon as they finished. Always and always they leave, that is of what they think.

I was here 4 years, before which in Germany: Wiesbaden „Kur-Orchester" in the summer and at the Opera in Darmstadt (very fine) in the winter, Kapellmeister Dr. Fritz Schleichmann, you may have heard his name, a very famous conductor. I could never become accustomed to Sir Grampian after this. Of course it is different in England. The public will only something to look at. A musician can tell. I do not know what the other players think, because I never see them to have conversations. I can say nothing.

I studied before to begin my work at the Music-School of Winkelbergen, that is my home. Direktor, Prof. Dr. Heinrich Rumpfstengel, another great musician. He died in 1925 or 26,

I am not sure, but I could find out. My violoncell teacher was Georg Gimpelburger, also very famous.

If you wish more informations, let me know, please, so that I can come to see you. I shall be glad to speak.

With great respect,

KARL ZIMMERMANN.

9, ST. GEORGE'S ROAD,

MANINGPOOL, 14.

8. 10. 38.

DEAR SIR,

My connection with the Maningpool Orchestra is a very short one, as I joined it only last season, as second clarinet. I consider myself more than capable of playing first, but as my facetious colleague, Mr. Evans, was on the spot first, I had to be content with second place for the present. I am afraid I do not consider him a very good player, though I would not deny his competence, and I admit that it is sometimes a little galling to feel oneself subordinate to a musician who, as such, has much in his favour, perhaps, but whose unfortunate, would-be humorous manner is hardly that of a gentleman. However, one must be prepared for these things in an orchestra, and I daresay the fact that he was under Sir Noel Grampian at Harmsford-on-Sea may have something to do with the security of Mr. Evans's position.

Yours very truly,

FRANKLIN POTTER.

P.S. I have no theories about the murder, or perhaps I should say they are so elementary as to be hardly likely to interest a gentleman of your profession.

15, LARCHWOOD ROAD,
RAMPTOWN,
MANINGPOOL, IX.

7 oct. 1938.

SIR,

It is with pleasure that I give suite to your demande. I have not been long in Maningpool, only since 1934, but at Le Havre since a long time (1925). I play there 1er violon, but actually 2me, it is sometimes more interesting. I like very much to play here and find it lucratif and agreable. My admiration for Sir Noel Grampian was very great. It was not possible for me to always agree with his idees, especially not about French music, but he had what we say the élan vital. He was charming and we often spoke together. He like to exercice himself in French with me. Many of the orchestre did not like him at all, but this I could perhaps understand. For myself, I was content. Only I could never ceasse to say to him he did not play enough French music and could not understand sometimes his taste. He like better Tchaïkoffski than the elegant Saint-Saëns—incredible! And this abominable Richard Strauss! We call him grossier. It is like a revenge, this death, do you not think so?

Unfortunately I cannot say how it happen. I sit at the back of the 2mes violons, in front, besides Mlle Elsworth, a good person, not young or pretty, but I find her agreable. My place is before the harpe (2 harpes for that terrible Strauss) so I turn my back on that charming Mlle Gwendolen Jarvis—to my grieve. It does not seem polite. I repeat I know nothing what happen, because immediately I turn to Mlle Jarvis when it happen, to assist her, if necessairy. She is jeune fille, not strong, delicate, and I fear immediately the shock will be terrible to her. Only the other day, at a repetition (pardon, rehearsal), she faint for no reason, or we do not know. (One does not ask.) I was happy to have the presence of spirit to find a glass of water for her. I would have done this again, but it was a confusion and the poor Mlle Jarvis was not at all fainting, but almost that beautiful Mme Ghilligan; she is the wife of the Professeur of Music here, not in the orchestre, but she play when second harpe is needed, as in Debussy, "Prélude à l'après-midi d'un faune," Ravel, "Daphnis et Chloé," etc., so genial French works, I hope you know them!

I return to Mme Ghilligan. Need I say that for her I would also have procured water? Yes, to be sure! But my galanterie was too late. Already M. le Prof. Ghilligan was here to watch on his excellent lady—it is beautiful, so much dévouement. (Excuse me, I cannot find the English.)

This, Sir, is all I can say. I wish you very good fortune in your discoveries and beg you to accept the expression of my complete consideration.

FERNAND LABOUCHÈRE.

Monday, 10th October

4 G.s,
M'POOL.

10. X. 38.

DEAREST OF JULIAS,

I've interviewed a few people whose letters seemed to me
worth following up. But I can't say I find much in them to make me
"point an unerring finger at the culprit." They all have grievances,
but it's difficult to estimate the relative seriousness of their com-
plaints, and I can't help feeling that their frank airing of them is in
their favour. Hardly anybody seems to have admired N. G. except
our Gallic friend M. Labouchère, and his exceptional attitude
would in itself look fishy if his position at the back of the second
fiddles *and* in the front row facing the stalls did not make him as
good as impossible, even if N. G. *could* have turned so far round to
the extreme right as to be shot from "just a little to the left."

The fellow I don't trust is Gough, the third viola. His letter,
you will have seen, is disgruntled, but he does not vent his grievance frankly. Something rankled there. Well, I thought I'd better
give him a gruelling, and he was among those I asked to call. He
was mulish at first, but I think it was due to a lack of personality,
a singularly unfortunate provincial want of *savoir-faire* and that
desire to obstruct authority which is nothing more than a resent-
ful awareness of inferior manners and intelligence. With some
handling that may or may not have been tactful, but at any rate

happened to be suitable, he came clean readily enough about his resentment at having been sacked by N. G. I was not too unfavourably impressed either by his insisting again on the fact that his dismissal would not mean a very serious financial loss. I do think that was more the defiance of wounded pride than any wish to minimise a possible motive for murder.

What struck me as much more queer, though, was the shock I gave him, quite visibly, by asking the perfectly natural question why he should still worry about his dismissal, now the man who dismissed him was no more. Nothing had been done about it in writing as yet, Taplow told me when I rang him up, so that Gough is not now under notice at all, as he knew perfectly well, I could see. And yet he did not simply leave it at that, as he might quite well have done if he wanted to stop my asking further questions. If he'd merely said "thank you for pointing that out," there would have been nothing more to it.

But no, he went all dithery and became ten times as recalcitrant as he had been at the beginning, so that I had to extort further answers from him with a corkscrew. He began to blink and stutter, I am not sure whether naturally or artificially, but anyhow it delayed the information I was after until even my exemplary patience (you know it!) was exhausted. In the end I got it out of him that he got the sack at the suggestion of Dashwood, the principal viola, who had pointed out to Grampian that Gough was not up to orchestral work above the average difficulty. But I could not for the life of me make out whether the silly embarrassed state he worked himself into was genuine because he did not want to implicate Dashwood, or artificially worked up because he did want to implicate him, or again genuine because he was ashamed to confess that his incompetence had been so much as suggested. I think it was this last, for he very emphatically proclaimed his being an artist, more so than some people he could mention, that Mr. Dashwood could not possibly judge, as he did not sit at the same desk with him, that many eminent musicians (whom he forbore to name) had thought a lot of his playing, and so forth—as pretty an exhibition of injured vanity as you could desire, and somehow, I felt, not particularly well justified vanity. He is a feeble little sandy fellow and pathetically afraid of committing himself in any way. One minute he fumed over Dashwood and the next, afraid of having said too much, he went out of his way to express his admiration for him as a player. And so on. It took me a fearful time to get him going, and then even longer to stop him from rambling on and on. All that time is wasted, I'm inclined to think.

Here are a few more comments, much shorter, you'll be thankful to see, and neatly classified under names of my correspondents.

Eltham: Pompous and conceited, as you'll have gathered from his letter. Good at his job, I should say, but his professional dignity is so overdone as to be positively revolting. He stayed over an hour and a half, to my ever-growing dismay, and I found at the end that although he had come with the promise of a bagful of vital information and the most valuable theories, he had absolutely nothing to contribute, had seen, heard, felt, tasted, or smelt never a thing, and in brief—only it wasn't he who was brief—had come not at all because he wanted to see me, but because he wanted me to see him. Not a fool, by any means, nor such a pest as I have perhaps unfairly made him out; for in some ways I could not help rather respecting him and thinking him a personality. But he is a fearful sticker and time-waster, so much so that towards the end I had to become business-like almost to the point of rudeness to get rid of him at all. And then I knew nothing more about the murder, Grampian, the orchestra, Maningpool or anything else, and only—what I did not at all want to know, since it told me nothing that bears on my case—all about Mr. Constant Eltham, England's Prime Minister among orchestral leaders. I suppose he *can* play the violin: he says nobody else can.

Tufton and Dipton: I put these two letters into juxtaposition only because their signatures, thus displayed, may cause you some mild amusement. Otherwise nothing to remark beyond the fact that these two were both engaged at N. G.'s instigation and were therefore among the very few who had some reason to like him. But you see that Tufton did not *admire* him, even so, and he took part in the petition for N. G.'s dismissal. Dipton protests rather overmuch; he too was in the deputation, but now says he had no grudge. Both may have something to hide that happened at Harmsford. On the whole not much in it, I think.

Dashwood: What about it?

Miss Lamb: No wolf's clothing about her, I think. She is what her name suggests, don't you feel? Look at the address and see how carefully she indicates that she is adequately chaperoned. A bit of a chatterbox, I fancy, for which reason, if for no other, I refrained from getting into touch with her. Besides, she is quite unattractive! She as good as tells me so at the end. (Have I succeeded in shocking you?) But, being aware of the fact, and of N. G.'s consequent disregard of her, was she inwardly boiling with rage? I'll bear it in mind.

Grant: Very straightforward (? suspiciously so). Conscious of his professional dignity, which N. G. might have hurt. But that applies to so many of them.

Beckenham: Nothing in it, I think; but look at the remarks about his training in England, as distinct from Grant's about his in Germany. Funny cattle, musicians!

Spinney: Rather deliberately detached, perhaps. But Mr. Spinney was placed on the top tier, in an unlikely position.

Beardling: I did phone Allport 2976, and sure enough the gentleman was in the club, having one, or more, I should say, judging by the state in which he arrived. But perhaps I do him an injustice: it may have been sheer funk at having to face the Police that made him overstep the mark. Anyhow, he was decidedly jumpy, but not a bad fellow, I thought. Why is he more accessible at the club than at home? Not only, I gathered, because it is "some way out," at Shifton, where after all others of the players live too, but on account of some domestic infelicity; perhaps only a nagging wife, perhaps worse. Never mind.

Lovelock: Half an outsider, apparently. He conveys nothing to me at the moment and I have not seen him.

Evans: Him I did see. I confess it was mainly curiosity, I didn't know whether his "Detective in distress" was meant to be funny or impertinently sarcastic, or whether he was merely clumsy. (Some of these chaps are not particularly cultivated, you will have gathered, while others pride themselves inordinately on their cultivation.) Well, Mr. Evans does try to be funny. It was a bit queer. He is a heavy, jovial-looking, red-faced chap with a luxuriant moustache. He wants to be amusing and doesn't quite know when it's suitable and when not. The sort of fellow who'd try to be the life and soul of a funeral, and who'd then become huffily mournful and solemn on being shown that it didn't go down. When I had let him try one or two sallies, I reduced him to that sorry state of a thwarted buffoon, one of the most ludicrously pitiable plights of human nature, by letting him see that I was deadly serious about finding the murderer and giving him just the glimmering of a hint that he was not himself free from suspicion. You see, he had joined the M'pool Orch. for the 1935 season, at the same time as N. G., and a time at which several others had come from Harmsford; but he did *not* say where he had been previously, and I wanted to know. He had been at Harmsford!

Zimmermann: Letter mainly for your delight. I did not see him. I don't see people who would be "glad to speak"—about themselves, as this solemn Teuton would certainly have done. I've had enough of that sort of thing from Eltham.

Potter: Nothing in it, to my mind, except that it was he who told me that Evans came from Harmsford, which was useful, though I should certainly have asked E. anyhow. If Potter had a grievance, it was against Evans rather than N. G.

Labouchère: I could not resist seeing him, and he amused me vastly, and also annoyed me just very slightly with his airs of *homme de discrétion.* I wasted his time and he mine, but I deserve a little relaxation, don't you think?

Even and ever your

ALAN.

Tuesday, 11th October

1, GARCHESTER HOUSE,
SHIFTON,
NR. MANINGPOOL.

OCT. 9TH, 38.

DEAR SIR,

I am sorry if my reply to your request comes rather late, but I have had my Mother ill in bed and have been unable to settle down to anything and even to think about anything but household duties. Also, I have been very much upset by the dreadful happening at the last Symphony Concert, and hardly able to collect my wits to give you a coherent account. Even now, I am bound to admit that I can think of absolutely nothing that might help you to form your conclusions. But perhaps you have been able to do so without my assistance by this time.

My connection with the Maningpool Municipal Orchestra dates from quite a time back now. I joined it in Sept., 1932. Before that I did not play professionally, but as I am well up to standard, there is no reason why I should not earn my own living. Concerning Sir Noel Grampian, while wishing to speak no ill of the dead, I can only say that I never cared for him; but of course one has to take these things as they come.

Yours sincerely,

CATHERINE DOYLE.

12 SHIFTON MANSIONS,
RAMPTOWN,
MANINGPOOL.

9. 10. 1938.

DEAR SIR,

I regret to say that I cannot throw any light on the most unfortunate death of Sir Noel Grampian, under whom I have been playing for some years now, i.e. the whole of his time at Harmsford-on-Sea, and from the time of his appointment here, when I was one of the players from the Harmsford Orchestra engaged by the Maningpool Orchestra at his recommendation.

There is no need to point out that I was naturally very grateful to the late Sir Noel for having obtained me a post that has yielded me better returns than those at Harmsford, and afforded me the pleasure of continuing to work under him. There has been a good deal of criticism of Sir Noel in this city, but personally I have always found him pleasant to work with, perhaps because I am not a person who cares about making trouble. As for his conducting, to my mind it was magnificent.

Believe me,

Yours faithfully,
ABRAHAM COHEN.

15, ST. PAUL'S GARDENS,
MANINGPOOL.

9 octobre, 1938.

DEAR M. INSPECTOR,

I regret my inability to tell you anything, and my writing in English is so bad that if you would permit me to write in French of to see you, I would be under great obligations. But I know nothing, absolute nothing!! But I will tell all I know when I can see you of write in French. I was born at Gand and study under the great Ysaÿe. Never will I forget this! I was in Maningpool since the before-last year.

Accept, M. Inspector, my sincere salutations.

GEORGES OOSTERMANS.

17, BRANSTON DRIVE,

MANINGPOOL, 3.

9th Oct. 38.

DEAR SIR,

As deputy leader of the Maningpool Municipal Orchestra (I share the first desk with Mr. Constant Eltham and frequently lead the concerts during one of his illnesses or other absences) I feel it incumbent on me to voice to you a theory of my own I have formed on the murder of Sir Noel Grampian, although I need hardly explain that it would have been quite impossible for me actually to *see* anything, as I was playing at the time. But I am convinced in my own mind that nobody in the orchestra could possibly have fired that shot. It would have been quite impossible for anybody to do so foolhardy a thing, and in my opinion it is waste of time to look for an explanation of that kind. What I feel sure happened is that somebody was concealed in the organ console, which was unoccupied that evening and is, as you may have noticed, screened on the side of the audience by a wooden partition. It would have been easy for anybody to hide there after the interval (anybody in evening dress, at any rate), as there were so many strangers present in the orchestra, men whom even we, the permanent members, did not all know so much as by sight. Personally I should have thought nothing whatever of it if any unknown man in a dinner-jacket had quite openly entered the green-room with me and afterwards appeared on the platform through one of those two upper doors leading down from the organ. Who could have hit upon such an ingenious idea it is, I am afraid, for you to discover, but I am perfectly certain that you will find my theory to accord with the facts, if indeed you ever solve this extremely difficult problem. If I have contributed ever so little to that solution, I shall, of course, be delighted.

Believe me,

Yours very truly,

FRANCIS J. HOLCOMBE.

2D, REPPINGTON MANSIONS,

ELECTRIC STREET,

MANINGPOOL, 4.

9th Oct. 1938.

DEAR SIR,

I must apologise for being a little late with my report, but I have been trying in vain to think of some explanation of the murder. Unfortunately the case still mystifies me completely, and I can only hope that you will be able to solve the matter without my assistance.

If I can be of any help at all, I shall willingly place myself at your disposal at any time, if you will kindly let me know. Meanwhile, I need only say that I have been in the orchestra here (2nd flute) for five years (this will be the sixth). I am rather worried wondering what is going to happen now, as we have no conductor, and shall, I suppose, have to put up with visiting conductors for the rest of this season, which is never very satisfactory. However, we shall almost certainly do better from a personal point of view. Sir Noel Grampian's sarcastic and sometimes downright rude and overbearing manner has been a great trial to us all. There was not a single member of the orchestra who did not cordially dislike him.

Yours faithfully,

J. W. ALSWORTHY.

MUSICIANS' CLUB,
MANINGPOOL.

9. X. 1938.

SIR,

In answer to your inquiries, I can only say that I am unwilling to go into any questions connected with the murder in writing, or to commit myself to any other statement except the following particulars about myself:

I play third horn in the Orchestra, which I joined the season before last. I was at Llanfawnwy until then, but am not Welsh, a native of Lancashire, and learnt music in my home town, Blackpool.

If you wish for any further information, I am quite willing to be interviewed, but I cannot take the risk of putting any theories or personal feelings in writing. Not that I have any.

Yours truly,

F. J. BETTERING.

4, CAMPDOWN STREET,
MANINGPOOL.

Oct^{ber} 9th.

DEAR INSPECTOR HOPE,

I have not been well, otherwise I would have written before. This business has quite knocked me flat and I have not been able to think strait since. I wish I could tell you who did it, Sir, but as I was only saying to a man at the Club yesterday evening, over a spot of something, I don't know from Adam. I should like to help. Sir N. G., as we often called him, if not worse, was a fair specimen, that is all I know. I always said something was coming to him, only last week at the Club, and many times before. I play trombone and have done here one way or another since a youngster. I am M'pool and never been out of it profesionnally. It is thirsty work, if you ask me, Sir.

I beg to remain, Inspector,

Yours faithfly,
GEO. COOK.

33, ST. GEORGE'S ROAD,
MANINGPOOL, 14.

10th Oct., 38.

DEAR SIR,

I regret not having written to you before, and I did not think that you would regard the matter as of so much importance as to insist on letters from those who have nothing to tell. Neither did I feel inclined to bow to "authority" by hastily and servilely answering to what I regard as an unwarrantably peremptory order. My principle is not to obey orders if it can possibly be avoided. I am proud, Sir, to call myself a Communist! As such the life and death of a man like "Sir" N. G. can be of no possible interest to me. As a knight he represented a system of Society which I am bound to abhor, and as a man he hardly existed for me, except when his offensive manner or his poor musicianship became too flagrant to escape notice. I should not in the least mind being answerable for his death, if I could feel that an isolated occurrence of this sort could have advanced the Cause; but as we must obviously wait for a more wholesale extermination of the vassals of capitalism, I can only dismiss this incident as in no way affecting me.

Yours truly,

W. G. DEANERY.

c/o St. Stephen's Vicarage,
Grafton-on-the-Water.

Oct. 10th, 1938.

Dear Sir,

Please forgive me for not answering your inquiry earlier, but I have been away for a few days, trying to recover from the shock of that dreadful evening. I am now more or less myself again and able to think more or less coherently; yet I fear it will take me a long time to get over this appalling experience. The worst of it is that it is all so mysterious, and if only I could feel that I could be of the slightest help to you, I assure you that I should not rest for a moment. If you wish to dispose of me in my spare time, I shall be only too glad to assist you in any way I can. I can type quite nicely and even know a little shorthand, which can never hurt an artist, even if Music naturally comes first. I also have more than a smattering of French, which enabled me to offer my services as interpreter to my neighbour (in the orchestra, I mean; we actually live a long distance apart), M. Labouchère, when he first came to England. But he said he preferred to battle with the intricacies of our language by himself, as he would overcome them more quickly that way. It was brave of him, I thought, and I suspect that he was chivalrous enough to wish to save me trouble.

I need only add, for the moment, that I studied at the R.C.M. (Royal College of Music) in London, played for a time in the South-East London Orchestra (partly amateur, but I was professional, of course) for the sake of experience; then I came to Maningpool, where I have relations—at least at Grafton, to be precise: the Vicar of St. Stephen's is my Uncle on my Mother's side, and I am quite one of the family. It was at my Uncle's suggestion that I tried for an appointment in the Municipal Orchestra here, and perhaps a little through his influence that I obtained it, although I think I may say that I am a competent player. Even Sir Noel, who had little use for women (as performers), once went so far as to admit it. I have been trying to form a string quartet, with M. Labouchère as viola (which he plays beautifully, as well as the fiddle), but little petty jealousies and other difficulties have so far prevented my doing so. However, I shall persevere.

Hoping that I have not wearied you with this long recital and that you may possibly find some use for me in your very difficult task, I remain,

Sincerely yours,

KATIE ELSWORTH.

ALAN HOPE, ESQ.
  59 DOUGHTY ROAD,
  SHIFTON.

Oct. 10th, 1938.

DEAR SIR,

I am sorry you had to send me a reminder via Mr. Taplow. The fact is that I could not quite make out what it was you required; but I think I had better set down the bare facts, and then, if you desire any conjectures and will kindly let me know, to ask if you will see me.

My engagement here dates from the season of 1935, but although I came at the same time as Sir Noel Grampian, it was not at his suggestion. I doubt whether he would have cared to have me, if he had had a say in the matter, as we had some fairly high words at Harmsford once or twice, where I was with him, and remained until I came here. Nor was I very anxious to play under him again, but it meant an improvement in my finances and I could not very well offend the gentleman at Harmsford who recommended me to the Committee here, where he had an influential friend. He has a good deal of influence himself, for that matter.

Trusting that I may hear from you if I have not said enough, I remain,

Yours truly,

ARTHUR M. REPTON.

P.S. I play third flute and piccolo here, as the case may be.

"Brownie Nook,"
Fillingham Gardens,
Maningpool.

10th October, 1938.

Dear Sir,

Kindly accept my apologies for not letting you have the required particulars earlier. I am afraid I have nothing to say about the murder. Nobody liked Sir Noel Grampian much, but it is unusual to kill anyone for that reason, especially in such a spectacular way. In my opinion it must have been the act of a lunatic.

I played first oboe at Harmsford, long before Sir Noel came to that place, and I stayed there after he had left. I came here when he took up the conductorship, and for the present play second oboe, which is still better than the Harmsford job, though of course less interesting. But Councillor Rossingham, at whose instigation I came here, knew from his friends here that Mr. Simmons, the present first oboe, was getting old and would be due for retirement soon, so that if I were on the spot, I should be sure to advance to his post. I therefore decided to accept.

If there is anything else you desire to know, I shall be pleased to write further.

Yours faithfully,

F. M. Best.

4 Georges,
M'pool.

11. x. 38.

Darling J.,

Here are the last of the orchestra letters. You've not by any means had them all, but quite a number of them are of no interest whatever. Just plain autobiographical facts and various negative references to the murder, free from conjectures, accusations, self-defence or other suspicious indications. I have kept the originals, of course, but did not want to burden my amiable assistants at the Police Station with unnecessary copying work or with a glut of food for thought that is sure to prove mere husks. I've had a bad enough time myself weeding out the improbable to want you to do the job over again. Still, I have included some of the more characteristic specimens, chiefly for your entertainment and such enlightenment as you may deem it interesting to have about the extraordinarily heterogeneous and socially unstable constitution of an orchestra. Did you have any idea that an assembly of musicians, whom we all think of, I suppose, as more or less alike, could contain such incompatibly different people? Well, there it is, and that's why I let you have some of the "documents" from players who were not in a position (physically speaking) to kill N. G. I hope you'll find them good reading.

Some of these last letters are from people who had not replied in a reasonable time and had to be reminded. They are all a bit questionable on that account.

I almost expected a wire from you this morning urging me to interview our Mr. Dashwood without delay. How you do trust me! But no, I had not forgotten him, or overlooked the fact that he must not be entirely cleared of suspicion merely because the revolver lay so openly and accusingly in front of him. That's the sort of psychological subtlety that drives Higgy crazy: he would have not only arrested D., but executed him on the spot, I verily believe, on that very evidence of the revolver, for he has great faith in the obvious, which I have learnt to distrust.

On the other hand, as in your blind confidence in that genius of a husband of yours you seem to have guessed, I have not entirely overlooked Mr. D. Actually I meant to act upon his generous offer to favour me with his conversation and observations without delay after my talk with the unsatisfactory Mr. Gough. But behold!—and don't shriek—when I tried to ring him up (he is one of the few members of the orch. who are on the phone) I was calmly informed by a female voice that he was out of M'pool and had not said when he would return. Tableau! It's nothing much to worry about, actually, for the Police here have tabs on all the orchestra, and D. complied with the order that any special movement should be reported to them. He has gone to play in the orchestra at the Knowlewich Festival and duly applied for permission to do so, as it is a long-standing engagement. He will be back on Friday, or if he is not, the Knowlewich Police will know the reason why, as they are looking after him, none the less tenderly because he is unaware of the fact.

And now for my second commentary (the final one, for all the players have now replied).

Miss Doyle: Nothing to report. I like her philosophical conclusion. If she takes these things as they come, she also puts them from her as they go, judging from her indifference to N. G.'s departure.

Cohen: He has been at Harmsford and should have known N. G. inside out. Then why this excessive admiration? Did you notice, by the way: several players say that nobody in the orch. liked N. G.; yet several others profess that they did. Again, why?

Oostermans: Included mainly for its quaintness. I may see him some time, for the fun of it. If he is really going to tell me all he does not know, it ought to be jolly.

Holcombe: Another one on his dignity. I have seen him and found it hard, without hurting his feelings unduly, to persuade him that his important discovery amounted to extremely little. He simply would not even try to understand when I showed him that the organ-loft, which I had fully considered long ago, is much too high up for that particular shot to have come from there. Also, anyone sticking his head over that partition to fire it would really have been a bit too conspicuous, much more so than he says any-one in the orchestra would have been. But, convinced against his will, he was of the same opinion still. I was rather sorry to prick this gaily-coloured bubble of his; he was so delighted with it, and he is a nice, sensitive chap.

Alsworthy: The end is curious, not because it throws any light on Mr. Alsworthy, but because it does so on others. What, not a single member who did not cordially dislike N. G.? But that makes Cohen's statement and those of one or two others who go out of their way to express admiration look still a bit more queerish-like.

Bettering: I did wish for further information, if only because I did not want this chap to get away with his silly quibbling and rudeness so easily. As I had expected, he was quite meek when it actually came to the point and, as he so comically observes at the end of his letter, he had nothing to tell. Then why all this pother?

Cook: This by way of diversion. Evidently the funny drunk of the party. "Not been well": he means tighter than usual.

Now we come to the laggards who would not perform their duties, and "all of whom are beauties."

Deanery: Oh, oh! That was my first reaction. But nothing here, I concluded: much too deliberately truculent. But I treated him to a long and uncomfortable interrogation, not at the hotel, the bourgeois comforts of which might have offended him, but at the chilly office of the orchestra. We parted quite amicably.

Miss Elsworth: Her I did *not* see. I dreaded her devotion to duty, much as, no doubt, M. Labouchère dreads her devotion to himself. But isn't it a revealing letter? Her statement that she has been away is a fib. We know she hasn't, because she reported at the office all right every other day. "Away for a few days" is merely a conventional effect, like "not at home."

Repton and Best: Oho! They both came here from Harmsford with N. G., but not at his suggestion. Well, well. And who is the gentleman at Harmsford? I did not know when I read Repton's letter, but enlightenment came with Best's by the following post. Or am I wrong? Did Mr. Rossingham not send *two* of the Harmsford players to M'pool? And if he did so, why? Rhetorical questions, but if you know the answers, tell me. Note, moreover, that Repton does not mention that he was under notice. Why?

Kiss the sweet babes, but don't as yet break it to them that their Daddy is the worst detective in England. For the first day or two of a case he knows nothing; then he knows so much that he can't see the wood for trees. I give it up. But only for to-night. Perhaps I shall *dream* the solution.

All my love,

ALAN.

Wednesday, 12th October

3, BACK OF 61,
BARROWS ROW,
WINTERDALE,
MANINGPOOL.

Oct. 11th.

Dᴿ SIR,

I hope as you will escuse me for writing re the Murder but I think I have a claw for you Sir making so Bold has to say, I Cleaned up under the Plattform this a.m. and notticed a Hole in it where I Stood looking strait at the Conductor Sir only of corse he wasnt there being Dead poor Gentleman and I shall be Pleased to Show it to you any Time Sir if Conveaniant to your Good Self

Yrs respy

MRS. HORSFALL.

Wed.

MY DEAR JU,

I went to see the estimable and respectful Mrs. Horsfall "this a.m." Incidentally I saw a part of the town that was new to me. Winterdale is far from resembling the spacious residential place of the Gillighans & Co., but though a slum now, not a depressing one, somehow, for all its soiled appearance. The Barrows Row houses must have been pretty once, like Miss Colling-Jones, but while she is still more genteel than shabby, it is just the opposite with them. They have that warm, irregular red of old brick (late 18th cent. I should say) and keep some of the more permanent original features: charming moulded architraves (if so pompous a term will do) over the windows, which themselves have yielded their original character to the common glazier, and over the doorways, where you'd expect a fanlight, an actual fan—one of those shell-like sandstone ornaments filling a semi-circular space most gracefully. But again, the doors are debased and hideously grained to present a low caricature of such oak as you see only in baronial halls at the pantomime. The street is drab, but not dull. It is too busy for that and has some funny little shops made out of the once self-respecting front sitting-rooms with a sort of casual and purely practical barbarity. It had been wet and then cleared up, so that the slate-blue tiles of the pavements shone against the light with the preternatural brightness of an Italian sky.

Mrs. Horsfall, as you may have gathered from her address, does not live in all this, but at the back of it. That is to say, when you have agitated a hysterical door-bell at one of those impromptu shops and made polite inquiries from a fat woman whose initial courtesy rapidly dwindles into a superb detachment, you go through a narrow passage between two of these houses and emerge into a place that partakes of the nature both of a backyard and a front-garden. There are little low fences and gates all round four small but quite friendly cottages, also of red brick, but of a newer and cruder variety. And if you have succeeded in detaching No. 3 from these, you have also found yours respy, Mrs. Horsfall.

I'm afraid I caught the good lady at a disadvantage and dragged her in a state of ruffled and panting embarrassment from some fierce household job. Obviously she had not expected her invitation to draw me to her home, but had hoped to act, decked out in all her finery, as my personal guide to the secret recesses of the Civic Hall. However, she got over her flurry and showed me into the parlour, into which the front door opened straight on to the flank of an old cottage piano, the most conspicuous piece of furniture, if only because it had a look of virginally disdainful disuse, with its spinsterish fretwork bosom backed by a piece of faded green—what? Was it bombasine, do you think? I hope so, for the sake of my description, which would somehow be incomplete without that.

Mrs. Horsfall so far defied convention as to have no aspidistra in the window and to refrain from "hastily dusting a chair with her apron." In fact—I am not sure, but to your more practised eye the room would, I think, have looked quite decently dusted already. The truth is that Mrs. H. had no reason to resent my call, and indeed she got over the shock long before I left.

Well, it appears that the space under the platform at the Civic Hall is used as a sort of store-room and that the door to it is always open. It is rarely cleaned, but Mrs. H. keeps her mops and pails there and has been told to give it the once-over now and again. But she has not held her appointment with the orchestra—as she put it—long and it was her first attack on the place yesterday. She hadn't "noticed it particular" before, it appears. Needless to say, she had the crime on the brain, and as she gave the dungeon a sweeping yesterday, she was struck all of a heap by that hole in one of the partitions in the platform. As a matter of fact there are three such holes, as I had indeed known from the first. Only I did not tell her so, not wanting to spoil her innocent pleasure at having discovered something the Police hadn't noticed.

As a matter of fact she did contribute something by inducing me to give my attention to a thing I had allowed to stand over. I hadn't even told *you* about it; but I may tell you now that, when I investigated the matter on the Saturday after the murder with the help of the doorkeeper, I found three openings, like little oval portholes, about 4" in height and 3" in width, some 6 feet from the ground, in that partition behind the violas (see sketch-plan of the orch. I sent you), one in the centre and the other two roughly behind and between the second and third and the sixth and seventh player. Well, that between the second and third looked rather promising, I was bound to admit. By standing on a packing-case (and there *are* packing-cases in plenty) it would have been quite possible to aim and shoot at N. G. through it; also, I think, *just* possible to jerk the revolver out through the hole immediately afterwards to make it land somewhere between the first and second viola.

The ideal solution, you will say. For a story, yes. But not for me! For do you realise, my good child, that it would again open up an infinity of possibilities, though against that we must bear in mind that we know positively that no outsiders left the hall after the shot (or don't we?). Also, I can't really see anyone hurling the revolver through that small hole with sufficient force to make it go so far. You try. You could *drop* it through easily enough to make it fall immediately below, *behind* the players; but to throw it in front of them, some 8 feet away, you would have to take aim several inches from the hole and could not be sure of clearing the space once in a dozen times, to put it very moderately. I tried it with my pocket-knife—a much smaller object—and succeeded only in my eleventh attempt in both clearing the hole *and* getting the knife to fall sufficiently far away. With a revolver it would have been at least twice as difficult. All this is far from conclusive, of course, and I am perhaps trying to argue myself out of accepting such theory, which would make the problem even more fiendish. I've got to bear it in mind, of course, and Mrs. H. has, I confess, brought it more urgently to my mind again.

By the way, those holes have not been cut (3 of them!) expressly for his fell purpose by the murderer. They have always been there and are a neat, regular carpenter's job. The door-keeper thinks they are there simply to admit some light and air into that otherwise quite unventilated space, and I've little doubt he is right, though they might have been some fanciful acoustical experiment, like the felt covering on the platform. One never knows with acoustics, does one? I could find out if it were worth while. It isn't. That felt covering, by the way, is another thing I didn't tell you about. It's a thin layer put all over the platform to reduce its excessive resonance. It would also, mark you, reduce the thud of a falling revolver.

But to return to Mrs. Geetumble. I took the opportunity of drawing her out a bit about the orchestra. Not that she knows anything much, but these people often get vivid impressions they are capable of reproducing with illuminating results of which they remain perfectly unconscious. Well, being pretty new to the place, she has not seen much of them, but has already formed the conclusion, at rehearsals which seem to coincide with her own Civic Hall activities, that musicians are a rum lot. Most of 'em is stuck-up, specially the ladies, it seems. The majority, if they meet her, will treat her like God's air, she says, and not only breathe her, but sniff her; some will wish her the time of day, just to say something, like; and two or three will have a word with her, if they feel like it. It seems to be a matter of mood. They were upset sometimes, and no wonder. She wished to speak no ill of the dead, let alone murdered, but that Sir Grampian had sometimes been on the rampage somethink chronic when they was practising.

Mr. Tufton, it appears, is the most affable. She didn't rightly know what he played, but had seen him blowing sideways into something like a huge fountain-pen. (Do you identify the bassoon?) And Mr. Cook (2nd trombone) was a proper funny one, he was, though she wouldn't say but what he took a bit more than was good for him. Little Mr. Lovelock, who blows one of them pipes, seemed glad to talk to anyone. Others had spoken to her, but she knew only their faces, not their names. One of them, with a fiddle under his arm, had come tearing down to her to ask for a glass of water for Miss Jarvis, who was feeling faint. Her that plays the harp. As pretty a piece of goods as ever you saw, and not above saying good-morning; but a proper little flirt, if you asked Mrs. H.—talk about bees round the honey-pot. Fair gone on her, some of 'em seemed. Always hanging round the entrance door waiting for her. More than one had asked her to lunch, and she had heard her refuse, very nicely, to go with that Mr. Dashwood. Even N. G. had offered to feed her, and been accepted, what's more, though nobody knew but she, who was at that moment having a word with Mr. Lovelock. And oh, the gent. with the fiddle had spoken with a foreign accent. (We know him, of course.)

But enough for to-day.

Ever thine,

ALAN.

Thursday, 13th October

13. X. 38.

DARLING,

As I write down the date, I reflect that the 13th is indeed an unlucky day. No, this does not mean that I have become superstitious: I'm not *asking* to be disqualified for my job. It simply means that *any* day is unlucky. The truth is, dearest, I am making no headway at all. You may ask if I am putting my back into it. Am I not? Yesterday, after all the probably futile Horsfall episode and my full account of it to you, I spent the rest of the afternoon and evening rushing round after the three trumpeters and the Belgian viola player who sat in front of that suspicious hole with our Mr. Gough, whom I did not particularly want to see again so soon. Of course not one of these good people is on the telephone or otherwise accessible except by a direct call at their widely scattered residences, and all Taplow could do for me in the way of getting hold of them was to put down those infernal addresses in some sort of order and connect them up with various bus and tram lines on a little map he drew for me. That at least saved me from blinding and blundering about the town like a blue-bottle in a meat-safe. But would you believe it? Having found M. Oostermans and the first trumpet, Holborne, at opposite ends of the town, I went to Beardling's place, not far from the latter's in the Birchton district, only to be told by a rather huffy Mrs. Beardling that he was not in and that there was no telling when he would be. My next visit was to Gorton's, at yet another end of a city which by this time seemed to me bigger than Vienna, and I heard there that Mr. Gorton would probably be at the Musicians' Club, which is, infuriatingly, a stone's throw from the Four Georges; not as grand as it sounds, but a place up a steep, clattering wooden staircase over a bicycle shop, like a dusty and cheerless tea-room from which the general public is excluded in favour of a number of dismally convivial, draught-playing, dart-throwing, have-another-Charlieing fellows who earn their livings at music in one way or another—theatre players, bandsmen and the lower orchestral ranks, mainly. And again would you believe it? I here not only found Mr. Gorton, but the elusive Mr. Beardling as well! Such is my lot. But no, I will not sink to a quotation from Gilbert—not yet; but you will find the appropriate passage in the second act of the "Pirates."

And the results? Oostermans, whose own lingo is clearly Flemish rather than French, since in conversation as in writing he persistently uses "of" for "or," was effusively polite, with that implication that politeness was rather a special concession than a habit which we used to notice in Brussels, you remember, still could tell me nothing, absolutely nothing, but evinced an astonishing amount of surprise when I mentioned the hole behind him and its possible significance. That may have been his natural—and national—sense of the dramatic, of course; but I wonder. His want of knowledge thereupon became positively vehement, if anything so negative can be that. As for his reaction to Dashwood, with whom of course he shares the first viola desk

(I am learning the technical terms, you notice), here again I was struck by a curious exaggeration. Their relations may be cordial, but I wonder why the deuce they should be quite as cordial as all that. It isn't human, somehow, when two people continually work in such close association. M. Oostermans is to be borne in mind, most decidedly. On the whole a decent chap, I thought, according to the Belgian variety of notions of decency, and he lives in quite pleasant diggings in a red brick and stucco house with bow windows, one of which is that of his sitting-room. All of this, the comfortable body of a landlady included, he rather goes out of his way to despise with the ostentation of one who probably has never been used to anything better. What he was used to in Belgium was probably merely different, perhaps not so good.

The trumpeters came next. Holborne showed every sign of contentment with his portion, which is that of having a wife who is anxious to please by servility and some by no means despicable remnants of earlier prettiness, and three nondescript children, two boys and a girl ranging from about seven to three, whom they were both pathetically eager to show off before me, with no very spectacular success, I'm afraid. Somehow I couldn't help feeling a little uncomfortably that they were both trying to impress upon me that this undistinguished offspring could be advanced as an excuse for something or other. I can't quite tell you what it was like, but it was as though they felt they had disarmed me once they had produced their progeny, whereby they were bound to good behaviour. The woman, who in ordinary circumstances would really mean it when she says "pleased to meet you" (people here don't say "how do you do," perhaps because it is a question nobody ever answers; has in fact long ceased to be a question), had fear in her eyes and was miserably anxious to please; which of course may have been attributable to a natural timidity in front of a policeman, or perhaps to a state of apprehension bred in her by the character of her trumpeter-husband. She has a way of furtively looking to him for confirmation before she does or says anything that seems to set him down as something of a bully. He is a great, hefty creature who might easily turn his profession to good account if the demolition of some modern Jericho were required.

He was inclined to cut up a bit crusty when I came to the point. With many a "look here, sir," he declared that he didn't know about anybody else, but that so far as he was concerned he would make no statement whatsoever without a lawyer. (He reads detective stories, obviously, unless he's learnt that dodge in real life some time.) I had to make it quite clear that he was no more under suspicion than anybody else, and a good deal less than some, but that I merely wanted to talk to those who might know something in order to clear things in my own mind; that those holes in the platform could not be disregarded, though I knew positively that the trumpeters could not have fired the shot, since they were back on the platform long before, and would obviously have chosen the "Battle" section for the crime if they had wanted to commit it. (I see I have not yet told you that three of the trumpeters [trumpets I—III], whom Strauss requires to play their fanfares behind the scenes at the beginning of the "Battle," did their bit of off-stage music under the platform, for which purpose those holes came in very useful.) That pacified him and relieved her; but I did not depart without being made to feel, somehow, that they were now completely unable to account for my visit at all. Well, perhaps they were right. I'm groping, darling, there's no doubt about that. And in so doing I feel like a worm. A worm, even, that is not likely ever to turn.

Messrs. Beardling and Gorton yielded me nothing whatever. They were playing darts at the club and seemed pretty far gone, both being unbelievably affable. I was immediately invited to "have one," chiefly because that would have been an excuse for at least two more for themselves, since I should have had to offer the next but one. Fortunately I could plead professional etiquette with a fairly good grace. As for the shooting, they as good as made fun of it, one saying that the something-or-other N. B. G. deserved all he got and that he himself would have been only too glad to have a pot at him, there being no harm in saying so, as he knew that he couldn't have, while the other something-else-well hoped ooever done it would get away with it, saving my presence, and he was sure even I agreed that nobody could say no fairer than that. And again, perhaps they are right.

During lunch.

A frantic telephone message from Beatrice, darling. Good thing I did not send this off. There will be more to add to-night, and I fear, from her tone and agitation, it may not be pleasant. She wanted to blurt it all out, of course, but I gave her no chance and rang off saying I'd be there at once. She little knows I'm going back to my excellent piece of Stilton first. That's partly because it's too good to waste and partly because it bolsters me up by giving me a spurious consciousness of maintaining a strictly professional attitude even when my friends become involved in a case of mine. For I gather from Beatrice that it's to do with the murder. Having dashed this off, I go to my duty, via Stilton.

Thurs. eve'g.

Be prepared for a shock, my dear. I am sorry, but I am most seriously apprehensive, though there is no need to worry unduly just yet. I have sent the revolver and the bullet up to the Yard for minute examination, in a rather vain hope that they will prove not to be related, though it's absurd to doubt this. In my experience criminals are neither so lucky as to find a weapon of the same calibre as their own lying about casually, nor so clever as to make instant use of such a coincidence and make it appear a pre-arranged scheme on somebody else's part. However, even if the weapon and the bullet are found to be united in legal wedlock, there is still plenty of chance that any one of thirteen people (at least)—that baleful 13 again, you see—may have used it.

But—brace yourself!—the revolver is Humphrey's. What Beatrice rang me up in such a frightful state about is that it is missing from the house. The worst of it was that she rang me about it in her first fit of panic while Humphrey was lecturing at the University, and that I got to the house and knew all about it before he got back, at tea-time. Beatrice had realised by then, I am quite sure, for she got more and more agitated, that she had acted disloyally by letting me know of the loss before Humphrey was told, and from his very peculiar manner, a sort of hurt and worried surprise, I could tell that he thought so too. I think B. knew that she was throwing suspicion on H., since she had told me she did not know whether he was aware of the loss or not, though fortunately she does not know that I heard from Labouchère how extraordinarily quickly H. had come upon the scene. H. himself was terribly upset, but of course the mere loss of the revolver and the idea that it could have been used by somebody or other through his carelessness in leaving it about was quite enough to disturb him violently.

He declared quite emphatically that he had not missed it and did not know that he had seen it for a month or so. It was in the top drawer of a desk, quite easily accessible, but also quite harmless, as it was never loaded and there were no cartridges near it or indeed anywhere in the house. It was an early possession, not used for years, and never since they came to M'pool. No effort of memory could get him anywhere near a definite idea as to when he had last looked upon the thing—consciously, I mean. He is very much the absent-minded professor and has no attention to spare for anything apart from his work and his wife. He said he opened that drawer now and again, but could not tell when he did so last. He is not even sure that he would have missed the revolver if he *had* opened the drawer since its disappearance; he might have simply imagined, without clearly formulating the idea at all, that it was in some other drawer, or he might not have given it a thought, if he happened to be busy with something else.

B., on the other hand, is at least quite clear as to when she last saw the revolver. She showed it to Miss Jarvis one day at the beginning of the season: you know, the girl who plays first harp and who so fascinates everybody, from Mrs. Horsfall to M. Labouchère and Mr. Dashwood, and was not without attraction to the ever-susceptible N. G., as Mrs. H. obligingly informed us. Well, it appears that B. was in the habit of inviting Miss J.

to come and practise the harp parts with her whenever a performance requiring two harps was impending. B., it appears, although an amateur, plays quite as well as "little Gwen," but the two of them find it easier to co-ordinate their two parts, which B. says often need working in very accurately together, if they have practised them side by side before the rehearsals start. Well, they knew at the beginning of the season that "Heldenleben" was coming on, and that the harp parts are difficult to play and to fit together. So Gwenny came to tea and they spent an hour or two on the job. They practised in the drawing-room, but went into the sitting-room-study after tea because B. wanted to give Miss J. a small cheque, as she always does on these occasions, insisting, in her kindness of heart, that after all Miss J. was giving her professional services. They are quite good friends otherwise, although I understand Gwenny is not quite up to Gillighan standards.

Now B., after getting her cheque-book out of the locked middle drawer of the desk, casually went to the unlocked one with the revolver in it, she hardly remembers whether with the intention of showing it to Miss J. or not: it was one of those haphazard actions one performs by the dozen day after day without clearly making up one's mind about them. (Or so she says, and it's perfectly credible.) Anyhow, show the revolver she did, merely because it happened to be there. "My dear, have you ever seen my husband's dinky little pistol?", she'd probably say, not knowing the difference. "It's quite all right, Gwenny, it's not loaded. Hasn't been used for years. But it's pretty, isn't it? My husband showed me how it works once: like this, I think. Don't be afraid, it won't go off." And so on. Then she put it back, and off went Gwenny with her cheque. *And* with the revolver? No, of course not. But I am always sceptical when people say "of course" quite so readily. So I asked further questions, only to find that B. was by no means as sure as all that. She had only said "of course" because she had not expected Miss J. to do anything of the sort. Why should she? But, come to think of it, she had gone upstairs to put her hat on before she went and B. had gone back to the drawing-room; and when Gwenny returned to say good-bye, she might quite well have slipped into the study first. Only, again, why should she? Why indeed? Most likely she didn't, but I am going to tackle her about it without delay. I can't visit her at her diggings or ask her to come to the 4 G.s (said he reassuringly), lest some person of Mrs. Horsfall's imagination should count me among the bees round the honey-pot; but Taplow has got her to come to the orchestra office at 11 to-morrow, and I shall be there, very eager indeed, but only professionally so, I trust. Think hard of me and guard me from a sticky end!

I love you till 11 a.m., Oct. 14—and thereafter.

In other words ever and ever yours,

ALAN.

P.S. How about my standing Sunday invitation to lunch at the G.s'? I can't possibly go next Sunday, unless I can clear my mind entirely of any afterthoughts connected with that revolver. Whatever happens, it is bound to be a factor in the case. Somebody must have fired it, since it was fouled and still warm from a quite recent shot, and if somebody did not pinch it... but let us go gently.—I am very apprehensive and have that hollow feeling in the pit of my stomach. If I write flippantly, it's because I don't want to worry you. Yet I know you've never thanked me for sparing you, bless you. So here goes: I am worried, *worried,* worried.

Friday, 14th October

4 Georges,
M'pool.

14. X. 38.

Dearest Ju,

I've just had my lunch, *not* taken in the company of Miss Gwendolen Jarvis. You may breathe again. She is a pretty and quite charming little thing, but not my cup of tea: one of the china-blue and gilt-edged kind, frail as M. Labouchère so admirably suggests, rather ready to cling in an emergency of a practical or emotional sort, but also to take the "oh sir, how could you?" attitude in another, I should say. On the whole stupid, but quite able to turn even that to good account on first acquaintance, and quite incapable of committing a petty theft for the purpose of taking part in a scheme for murder, except perhaps under some special pressure or urged by some exceptional emotional exaltation.

The bare suggestion that she could have taken the revolver produced a wide-eyed and wounded astonishment in her—in fact a perfect specimen of the "sir, how could you?" reaction. The notion that she might have returned to the study before she said good-bye to Beatrice utterly bewildered her. Why should she? Oh, I ventured, she might have thought Beatrice was still there. No, she knew she had gone into the drawing-room. Anyhow— this with some faint glimmering of spirit—she loved Mrs.

Gillighan and would never dream of doing anything of the sort to her. I believed her, and said so. This restored her confidence, and so far we got on all right.

The date of her visit to B., which the latter could not remember exactly, turned out to be Monday, Sept. 12. Miss J. could not at first recall it either, but she knew it must have been during the week of the first Symphony Concert, which took place on Thursday, Sept. 15, as she had got back to M'pool from her home only on the previous Saturday, the 10th. Eventually she remembered quite definitely that it was the Monday, for some trivial reason not worth recording.

You remember that Beatrice had not seen the revolver after showing it to Gwenny (no, I don't call her that to her face, darling) and that Humphrey had no idea whether he had seen it or not. We may therefore take it that it disappeared some time between Sept. 12 and Sept. 29, the day of the murder; and if you ask me when, I say that I do not know, but plump very naturally for the day of the deputation to Humphrey, Sept. 14, when no fewer than thirteen members of the orchestra were in that very room (purposely received there by Humphrey, I fancy, because the atmosphere is rather more business-like than that of the very pleasant drawing-room). The drawer, as you know, was unlocked.

Now you will object to this, perhaps, that there is safety in numbers in such a case; that any one of thirteen people would find it very much more difficult to abstract a revolver from a piece of furniture in another man's house, where he has no right to open drawers, than a single person would have done at any time during these seventeen days. Well, I grant you this most graciously. But listen. Some at least of the thirteen players knew about the revolver. For I was brute enough to ask the tender and yielding Gwenny whether the deputation *could* have known it, and the tone of paternal earnestness rather than downright severity, with perhaps a hint that I was asking a purely rhetorical question concerning things I already knew all about, surprisingly reduced the little thing to tears. Yes, she had been naughty, but would not so far distress her Uncle Alan as to tell a lie. Yes, she had told several people in the Civic Hall green-room about the revolver, at the rehearsal on the Tuesday morning after her visit to Beatrice, Sept. 13. (She had nothing to do at the first symphony concert, as there are no harp parts in the Mozart, Schubert and Tchaikovsky Symphonies, but went there to see the gang after their return to M'pool.) She could not remember exactly who had heard the story, but Mr. Eltham, the leader, Mr. Beckenham, the first flute, Mr. Dashwood and she thought Mr. Tufton had been there, also several of the ladies, which—*entre nous*—would account for the rapid spread of the tale, unless male musicians are, as I suspect, equally good at gossip. The four men she mentioned, you notice, were all principals and therefore members of the deputation. But of course the information may, and indeed must, have gone much farther than that. We once again have a wonderful range of goods to choose from!

When the little lady had dried her tears, I pressed her still further. (I speak purely metaphorically.) It seemed to me a pity to tear myself away before I had discovered how she envisaged her secondary functions in the orchestra in the capacity of honey-pot. On the whole she rather enjoys them, I found, though she doubtless does not think she told me so. But she is far from being a brazen hussy, and though quite ready to be taken to lunch after rehearsals by all and sundry—anybody who can get in first to book her, almost—I think she gets rather frightened if she finds that she is arousing any serious passion, though a little of it agreeably flatters her, as is only natural, and she can do with any amount of adoration and, I daresay, mild flirtation.

When I asked her who had taken her to lunch, she said "Oh, lots," and on asking who had done so more than casually, I found that Sir Noel himself had taken her to the new Langdon grill-room twice since the new season started, but that she had rather disliked being seen with him and talked about in connection with him, as she had heard many stories of his always going about with girls, and there had been worse rumours, she understood. She really preferred lunching more modestly with M. Labouchère, who was always friendly and almost fatherly, though a little too much given to patting her hand—indeed he had even kissed it once or twice, but discreetly, when nobody was looking, and that was only his foreign way, anyhow. Or with Mr. Holcombe or Mr. Crawley, who were both nice and never silly, or hardly ever.

Mr. Dashwood asked her, too, but she did not always accept. She liked him, of course, he was so interesting, but he was married and she did not think it quite right, and she was afraid he was really too serious about everything, herself included. Indeed, she had recently had reason to fear that he was really falling badly in love with her, and of course that would never do, though she must admit she did like him very much in many ways. She was afraid she had upset him dreadfully more than once, especially by lunching with Sir Noel when she had refused to go with him, and even once simply by trying to be kind to poor little Mr. Lovelock, about whom surely nobody need be jealous, he was such a funny little man, almost a dwarf, and quite unattractive; but there was no need to be rude and stand-offish, and she could see no harm in being nice to him occasionally, even if it did upset other people, if they were so silly and could not see that she made a difference between him and them. It was bad enough for Mr. Lovelock, always being teased by some of the other players, who weren't all gentlemen by any means.

Need I give you more of Gwenny's artless but not uninstructive prattle? Hardly. You have judged by this time that, though she is a ninny and an arrant flirt, she is by no means a heartless minx and probably quite harmless in a stupid, unimaginative way that can as a matter of fact do quite a lot of harm. She has neither the grit to keep her admirers off nor the resolution to make her choice among them and then stick to it, with the result that she keeps things seething rather enervatingly among a good part of the male section of the orchestra, and perhaps among the female part too, where no doubt there is a good deal of jealousy and embittered comment. I should be surprised if the estimable but "not young or pretty" Miss Elsworth, for instance, were cordially devoted to Miss J.

As, however, I am to you.

Yours,

ALAN.

Evening.

I had already done this up for the post when I discovered, on ringing up the house of Mr. Dashwood, whom I am more anxious than ever to see, that he had not returned home, though he was due to-day. I did not tell the household that I was quite well aware of his having been at the Knowlewich Festival and that it finished last night, and they still saw fit to pretend that they knew nothing of his whereabouts and could not tell when he would be back. I can't think why, unless it's simply a pose. (You can make that sort of thing sound so grand, can't you?) I confess I am growing a little uneasy about this fellow and about my theory that a man who looks so much like being a murderer can't possibly be anything of the kind. However, the K'wich Police assure us on the phone that they have got him tethered and that he has arranged to spend another night at the hotel in K., for no known reason. Whatever that reason may be, they will see to it that he does spend it either there or under their own immediate care, and he will also be accompanied (unknown to him) to-morrow—home or whithersoever he may choose to proceed. More of this anon. It ought to be interesting, every-how, as they say here.

P.S. Very clever of you, once again, darling, to have spotted that point in Tufton's letter. True, he says that he was playing when the shot was fired, and as *you* say, how did he know exactly when it was fired, when even the doctor couldn't tell? And as you say further, he came from Harmsford. It will bear looking into, and I'll keep it in mind. Thank you so much, Angelic One.

Saturday, 15th October

4 G.s,
M'POOL.

15. x. 38.

LIGHT OF MY LIFE,

(but not, unfortunately, on my investigation!) I am immensely, passionately grateful to you, darling, for your long and most interesting letter, and if your conjectures do not really elucidate anything very much, they do nevertheless help enormously, (a) because they make me think things out afresh and (b) because they show, I flatter myself, that your anxiety to help in speeding the show up has something to do, however remotely and subconsciously, with an obscure desire on your part to have me home again some time this side of Christmas. Well, I shall be, but whether this side of Christmas 1938 is another question. However, I have hopes. I can dimly begin to see various matters taking shape and others quietly dissociating themselves from the case, however important they may have looked at first. In fact I am now on the verge of that period of mystery which always exasperates you so much, but invariably, if I may say so, precedes Inspector Alan Hope's brilliant solution. (Pride before the fall—of the criminal, I hope, not myself!)

I see you do suspect Humphrey. My dear, I am so sorry, for I did not want to convey to you that there really were serious grounds for that, though in my own mind I had the gravest misgivings. Why, as you say (for we may now as well have it out), was Humphrey on the spot so quickly after the shot to stand by the faltering Beatrice? It isn't at all easily explicable, for you are quite right in supposing that he must have been in the auditorium during the performance, not behind the scenes. Your question whether he could have been under the platform, having got there after the three trumpeters had left and gone back into the orchestra, is distinctly disturbing, I admit, and we have seen that the shot *could* have been fired out of one of those holes and the revolver just conceivably flung through the hole afterwards.

But consider two things: first, Humphrey would surely have gone anywhere rather than on the platform after that shot, unless of course his love for his wife proved stronger even than caution or else he was seen by an attendant and justified his presence behind the scenes by a desire to look after Beatrice; secondly, he had no grudge against Dashwood or any other player, so far as I can see or imagine, strong enough to make him wish to incriminate him, and he could have left the revolver safely enough, for the time being, somewhere among the junk in that Black Hole of Calcutta under the platform: in an empty packing-case, for instance, or behind one of those large bales in which, I was told, an old carpet off the Civic Hall floor is rolled up in strips pending its sale at second hand, a sale now long deferred and becoming more and more problematical. I really don't think you need worry unduly about Humphrey, though I bear him in mind, of course. After all, what is his motive? Ridding a sister-in-law on whom his adored wife dotes of a husband who is admittedly unsatisfactory, but without whom she is able to live, if not reasonably happy, at least not in any sort of economic distress. Is it strong enough? No, no.

But then, again, have we as yet discovered *any* strong motive? Ask me several others. We have not. All the same, definite suspicions are forming themselves in my sluggish brain. Among them our Mr. Dashwood was playing lead last night, in fact until this morning. But I have now degraded him to the part of a super, though not sent him off the stage. Don't be disappointed, darling, but he turned up at home this morning, duly escorted by the Knowlewich Police, and professed himself delighted to accept my invitation to an interview at the Four Georges, which was awaiting him. His wife, having continued almost to the last to keep up the absurd fiction of ignorance as to his movements, became a case of "Fain would I change that note" when I tactfully conveyed to her how unfavourably a man impresses himself on the Police in a murder case if he shows any reluctance to meet inquiries or to give information. She had no doubt that Mr. Dashwood would dash to my hotel the moment he arrived from K., which, she had heard that morning, would be by the 10.45. He was closeted with me by 11.35. Good work.

Better work followed. I've at last got Mr. D. where I want him. It was comparatively easy, considering the enormities I had to wheedle him into confessing. You have seen how he prides himself on his superior intelligence. This served me well, for I was able to take the line of "you and I understand," "between two men of the world," "safe with the Police if you have nothing to hide," &c. I began by saying that I had no intention of questioning him as to his reasons for that extra night at K., though as man to man I might say that, whatever it was, I should be sure to take a charitable view, only fools imagining people to be infallible. He lapped it all up with delight, and I can't help thinking that he would have been quite sorry if I had failed to suspect there was something in it, even if actually there wasn't. All this, by the way, was accompanied by a double whisky, followed in due course by another. I got him more and more mellow, and from the hotel episode we came by a natural transition to a veiled confidence about domestic trouble, at which indeed it had not been difficult to guess from the voice on the telephone. I then expatiated (during the second double Scotch) on my training in the understanding of human nature, which of course duly aroused that ever-alert intellectual curiosity of his. I said that N. G. was a fascinating specimen to me, talked about his philanderings, and gently brought in Miss Jarvis. At which he bristled, declared that N. G. had behaved like a swine in trying to ensnare that helpless little girl, that there were certain things which were different, and so on.

This was the dramatic moment. Having him as mellow as a medlar, I suddenly pounced with the observation that he was too intelligent not to know that I must have got him there with a definite purpose, to ask him some very serious questions which I hoped, since I had taken a real liking to him, he would be able to answer to my satisfaction. I told him that the revolver had disappeared from the Gillighans' house after Miss J. had seen it there, and did he think she had taken it? Indignant denial, as I had expected. Then who had taken it? Obviously one of the deputation, a statement he did not have the presence of mind to dispute. Indeed I left him no time, but went on immediately to point out that unfortunately suspicion fell in the first place on himself, as he had asked the Professor for a score of "Heldenleben," which had to be fetched from upstairs, and that only during Humphrey's absence could the revolver have been taken out of the drawer.

And (a shot in the dark) he, Dashwood, was standing nearest the desk. My dear, this was astonishingly, staggeringly successful. I had at the most expected a lead to somebody else, possibly some false or random accusation. But no, out tumbled a nervous, fidgety confession, curiously mingled at the same time with that odd predilection of his for imparting interesting information. Once he had got over the first shock and adjusted himself to the necessity of taking this new turning, he really quite enjoyed telling me about it; and, perhaps thanks to my having begun by establishing an atmosphere of gentlemanly confidence, which he somehow seemed to take to be mutual, though I had not told him a thing and he was spilling information all over me, he was perfectly frank about it all. Not that, according to him, he had anything to fear, but I doubt whether without his extraordinary conceit, and perhaps without the double double Scotch, I should have got such a story out of him.

And here it is. Yes, he did pinch that revolver. It was quite easy, it appears. Not that Gwenny had said exactly where it was, and of course he had not been able to ask questions; but he had simply kept near that desk all the time, and knowing that the thing was in a top drawer, had contrived to locate it even before Humphrey had left the room. The middle one, with Beatrice's cheque-book, as we know, he found locked. The one on the left, which he managed to open while the others were gazing out into the garden, on which he himself had complimented Humphrey in order to distract their attention, was not what he wanted. So it must be the one on the right, which he left until Humphrey had gone upstairs and he had drawn the men's attention to Grinston's Academy portrait of Beatrice at her harp, which hangs in the study and about which I have no doubt he had some particularly interesting point to make that sent them all across the room with their backs to him.

He was able to make this amazing confession to me because, he said, he had not after all shot N. G., though he had fully intended to do so, if he could find a suitable opportunity. He had not even bought ammunition for the revolver, not knowing exactly how to set about that sort of thing (and it *is* surprisingly difficult to the amateur murderer who has no licence). After going about with the wretched thing for several days and finding it more and more of an incubus, he decided to get rid of it. But again he came upon those queer difficulties and came to the conclusion that nothing is harder than to rid oneself of an unlawfully acquired and in itself unlawful object secretly. Presently he hit upon the idea ("very interesting, Inspector!") that it could be got rid of much more easily if he made no secret of it at all. So when they were all washing in the men's cloakroom after a rehearsal, or at any rate fifteen or twenty of them, he just calmly put it down on the marble shelf above one of the wash-basins, said "Hullo, what's this?" He picked it up again, exclaimed "Who the deuce leaves things like this about?" and everything was perfectly all right. If anybody was now under suspicion, they all were, and every one of them, to every one else, rather more than he. But of course there was no cause for any particular suspicion at all. Nobody knew that there was going to be a murder, Lovelock said it wasn't loaded anyway, and after it had been handed all round and fooled about with for a bit with mock threats of instant execution and so forth (you remember about the traces of mixed fingerprints on the criss-crosspattern), Gough suggested that they had better leave the thing where Dashwood had found it (oh, oh!), which they did. Who went back to retrieve it afterwards, whether Dashwood himself or any of those people, or whether anyone else found it later, is what I should like to know, but cannot find out by direct inquiry, for I am not likely to get another confession of the Dashwood variety. Even one is almost too good to be true. Nevertheless, I vow I have told *you* the truth, dearest, so far as I know it. What I am not telling you is all I think, for, believe it or not, that would be a waste of my time, since 90 per cent. of those ideas will inevitably have to be discarded again. They are just whirling through my mind like ballet dancers in the final ensemble, except that they will not yet form themselves into a pattern and there is, alas! nothing final about them.

Interval

Am I to scrap all the foregoing? Perhaps not. Some of it may still give us a lead. But it is all fantastically modified, and you'll be glad to hear it, I know. My dear one, I have had a summons to the Central Police Station, expected ever since last night, where the report about the revolver and the bullet had just come in from the Yard. You may be shocked to hear that they have been living together in sin ever since the Police took charge of them on the night of the murder; otherwise no doubt you'll be immensely relieved. So am I. Think of it: I shall be able to go to lunch at Rookdale to-morrow after all. But that's only, so to speak, the outward and visible symbol of my pleasure. What I really rejoice over is that Humphrey's revolver had simply nothing to do with the murder; that is to say, with the actual shot and the actual death of N. G. That shot came from some other weapon of the same calibre, and Humphrey's dinky little toy is merely among the trimmings of the case.

Did I say rejoice? Of course I do as a private individual. But as a policeman I am more than ever up against it. What now, indeed? I am faced with the task of going all over the case again, of facing heaven knows how many more interviews, of searching for I don't know what. That second weapon, where on earth is it likely to be? You see, the locals were so sure—and quite reasonably, too—that the shot had come from the revolver on the platform that they never thought of searching anybody. Why should they? I could so easily say that *I* should have searched, but although I do think so now, I can't really be too sure. It's so easy to be clever after the event.

Lord! I must rush to the *M'pool Telegraph* office before it closes. Excuse me. I'll resume this once again and tell you what I want there. It gets madder every minute.

Later still.

What I wanted at the *Telegraph* office were some more cuttings. You'll think I've gone crazy, and you're quite right. But, encouraged by your ingenious findings in Ransom's newspaper stuff, I went through it again and twigged something that has sent me to the paper's files. And behold! But more of that to-morrow, when I will write another budget and enclose the cuttings, with which I must meanwhile, at once, to-night, by hook or by crook, confront Ransom.

Meanwhile, here's another small matter I had better get rid of to-night, as I shall have a frightful lot to say to-morrow, I'm sure; for on ringing up Beatrice at once to reassure her, poor thing, about the revolver, I hear that Letty has arrived and is dying to meet me. The mortality among prospective "meeters" of B.'s acquaintance reaches positively alarming proportions.

Now for the matter in hand, which concerns another of your clever if perverse suggestions. No, my love, there's nothing in your theory about the three trumpeters who go outside before the "Battle" section, though you are right in reminding me that they did produce their far-off effect *under* the platform. You are quite right, too, in saying that the battle makes such an infernal row that anybody who wanted to shoot N. G. during the Strauss piece would, one would think, have chosen that part of it. Well, so would the trumpets, if one of them were guilty, and the fact that they missed this first-class opportunity shows, surely, that they are innocent. They would not have shot afterwards, from an unfavourable position, when they could have done so quite easily from under the platform. You have contributed something useful by actually eliminating them in trying to throw suspicion on them, and you may now take our second list (the one I sent you on Saturday* and cross out the *d* (for doubtful) in front of them and mark in *o* (for out of the question) instead. You see, they really had a first-class opportunity under the platform (the difficulty of throwing the revolver through the hole no longer matters, since the shot was fired by another weapon), and although no man is infallible, our medical evidence shows that the shot could not have been fired so early. A man cannot be wounded *mortally* and

---

* See page 70.

carry on conducting so long and during such strenuous music, and don't tell me that N. G. was not in the first place mortally hurt, but made the wound mortal by abnormal bodily exertions. That's too far-fetched to pass except in the very last resort. The doctor would have to be found incompetent, which is only just thinkable in the case of a Police surgeon.

The odd thing is that the greater we see the three trumpeters' opportunity to have been at the beginning of the "Battle" section (though the biggest row of drums and so on does not actually start until they have returned to the platform, J. R. tells me), the more certain can we be that they are innocent. For undoubtedly one of them would have shot then, if he had wanted to; and Taplow tells me, in answer to my inquiry, that the three trumpets actually did stand on packing-cases or something, each behind one of the holes, through which they could see the conductor's beat. Aha! But observe, darling, that the partition behind the violas curves in such a way that the three chaps playing behind the holes *could not see each other. Voilà!* If you can prove to me that the shot *was* fired at the beginning of the battle, you have as good as proved that the fellow at the hole between violas 2 and 3 did it, and that the other two knew nothing about it.

After these few hasty jottings (!) I can only say "good night," or rather "good morning," for I am well into Sunday now. I got hold of Ransom, but must go to bed and continue to-morrow. But he and I don't like each other so much now.

Lots of love,

ALAN.

Sunday, 16th October

Four cuttings from *The Maningpool Telegraph*

Monday, 19th September 1938

TO THE EDITOR OF
THE MANINGPOOL TELEGRAPH

SIR,

In his report of the Maningpool Municipal Orchestra's first Symphony Concert, your critic, J. R., has begun, without delay, launching virulent attacks on me once again, attacks which, although they are couched in more or less strictly professional terms, can only be regarded as personal, to use no stronger term. Not having the honour of J. R.'s acquaintance, which I may say he denied me the pleasure of making on what, I understand, he was pleased to call grounds of professional etiquette, I am unable to conceive the reason for his obviously violent dislike of me.

Such a situation being difficult to bear for any length of time, I am quite prepared to give your vitriolic contributor a perfectly sound basis for any future expressions of his spite.

I noticed this morning, at a preliminary rehearsal of my forth-coming performance of Strauss's "Heldenleben," that J. R. had availed himself of the usual privilege extended to the Press by attending this rehearsal. Kindly note, and convey the information to him, that I have given instructions to the officials of the Municipal Orchestra to see that he is in future excluded from these purely private functions, admittance to which is granted only by a courtesy for which we seem to be incapable of earning any return.

We are, of course, unable to refuse invitations to our performances to your valued journal. There, I am afraid, J. R. must do his worst, and I have no doubt that he will.

Yours faithfully,
NOEL GRAMPIAN.

NINE MUSES CLUB,
MANINGPOOL,
 September 17.

Tuesday, September 20

TO THE EDITOR OF
THE MANINGPOOL TELEGRAPH

SIR,

Sir Noel Grampian, in the peevish letter addressed to you from the shelter presided over by the Nine Muses, accuses me of writing adversely about his performances—which I do not always do, by the way—for the pleasure of indulging my personal feelings. Since, as he himself points out, we do not enjoy the felicity of each other's acquaintance, and that by my own choice, I utterly fail to see how he could imagine any personal dislike of him to have arisen. I am therefore forced to conclude that Sir Noel is incapable, not only of crediting me with any sort of professional detachment, but also of conceiving the bare possibility of his being wrong in anything he chooses to do in front of an orchestra.

Nobody would be happier than I, were it possible for me to share the exalted view Sir Noel takes of himself, but until I find myself honestly able to do so, I am afraid I shall have to continue giving you my views of his work exactly as they are. I am anxious to keep this dispute on a strictly professional basis: it is Sir Noel who is personal. He does not defend his work; he merely complains about mine. Why not try to convince me that the extravagant gestures to which he resorts in conducting really mean something?

As for his withdrawal of the traditional invitation to rehearsals, I regret it. They have often been interesting and instructive, if at times only negatively. But I shall not greatly mind enjoying a little extra leisure in future, though I fear I shall not employ it in cultivating the friendship of executive musicians, and I am quite capable of forming a judgment of a work or performance without any preliminary hearing. If Sir Noel suspects me of making up my mind from such a rehearsal as that of "Heldenleben" last Saturday morning, which was merely a run-through by the permanent orchestra, without the numerous extra players the work will require next Thursday week, he is accusing me of unprofessional conduct as well as of personal animosity.

Yours faithfully,

JASPER RANSOM.

ROOKDALE,
  MANINGPOOL.
    September 19.

Thursday, September 22

TO THE EDITOR OF

THE MANINGPOOL TELEGRAPH

SIR,

It is not for me to prove, as your critic would like me to do, what my "extravagant gestures" mean. It is for him to make up his mind about them, if the strictly professional judgment on which he plumes himself amounts to any real knowledge and taste.

I am, however, prepared to give him every possible chance. In order to allow him to watch me more closely than he has been able to do from the seat given him for the opening concert and in past seasons, I am arranging for tickets to be sent to him in future for two seats at the side of the lower gallery, over the first violins and facing my left side.

At the risk of suffering intense discomfort under his eagle glances, I take this step entirely in order to help him in his work and to offer him the proofs he requires in a manner that should remove all possible misunderstandings of my artistic intentions.

Yours faithfully,

NOEL GRAMPIAN.

15 ACACIA DRIVE,
    ROOKDALE,
        MANINGPOOL.
            September 21.

Friday, September 23

TO THE EDITOR OF

THE MANINGPOOL TELEGRAPH

SIR,

Sir Noel Grampian, now forsaken by the Nine Muses as well as by the last vestiges of fairmindedness, in spite of his protestations of good faith, proposes to let me listen to his next Symphony Concert from the worst possible position in the Civic Hall. For all his pretended courtesy, he is, of course, perfectly well aware that at some other musical function a year or two ago these very same seats were offered to me, and that I indignantly refused to write a notice of the concert in question (I do not write "reports," by the way) unless a place was given me from which an orchestra could be heard in its proper balance. (I say *heard*; but I daresay it surprises Sir Noel to be told that anybody should want to go to a concert in order to listen to music and not in order to look at him.)

The correspondence that arose from this dispute was published in your columns and the matter is public property. I happen to know from reliable witnesses that Sir Noel heard about it and agreed with me. I may thus leave it to your readers to judge whether his present action can really have been intended to assist me in my professional duties.

However, I shall not refuse the seats this time. I am bound to accept Sir Noel's challenge, since it comes in response to one of my own, and I shall in fact be very glad of the opportunity of watching him closely. The rest shall be on his own head, though I need not say that I am always open to conversion, for I prefer performances that I can honestly like, strange though that may seem to Sir Noel. But I do not think that his closer proximity to me will make his methods appear any more reasonable. I am afraid we shall both be "suffering intense discomfort."

Yours faithfully,

JASPER RANSOM.

ROOKDALE,
> MANINGPOOL.
>> September 22.

[This correspondence is now closed.—Ed.]

FOUR GEORGES,

MANINGPOOL.

16. X. 38.

MY DEAREST JU,

I now enclose the cuttings of the correspondence between Grampian and Ransom, for your edification. If they do no more than afford you a little light relief, they will have justified themselves. But there's more in them than that. J. R. was rather disagreeable when I called on him last night. In fact I think he had tried to make out that he was not at home; but somehow his wife and the maid between them bungled things over the telephone, and there was no getting out of it. He was distinctly uncomfortable, and very unconvincing when I asked him why he had not mentioned that quarrel with N. G. before or sent me the cuttings of the letters when I asked him for anything that had appeared in the paper which might have a bearing on the

case. Nothing better occurred to him by way of excuse than that
he thought only of the contributions he had made to the paper
as a critic, and that it was perfectly natural for him to overlook
letters to the Editor, which were not part of his actual work.
They were constantly being written, he said, and nobody paid
any attention to them, either in the *Telegraph* office or out of it,
and they were forgotten the day after the publication. I daresay
there's something in it, but N. G.'s caddish action was not a thing
to be lightly dismissed.

Well, the two seats offered to J. R. by the management for the
rest of the season, at N. G.'s instigation, were the last two at the
end of the balcony on the left. You will find them on the sketch-
plan of the orchestra I sent you, and you'll see that they are placed
directly over the first violins. J. R. occupied the second seat from
the end, and although the last seat too was his, nobody was with
him that night. His wife had developed a headache at the last
minute, he said, though when I subsequently tackled her about
it, before Ransom could make her say what he wanted, she told
me that she was not very musical and he had suggested to her that
she would not enjoy the Strauss. On the other side of him were
two more empty seats, he had to admit when I hinted that I would
find out from Taplow. So there he was, in single glory. The seats
in the only row behind him were also unoccupied, as nobody
likes to sit in that position unless they have to when the hall is
absolutely packed, which happens only, Ransom scornfully says,
when people don't go to hear music but to see some celebrated
musical performer.

Just to make a dramatic effect, I may perhaps remind you
that R. was seen to have his head buried in the score during

"Heldenleben," according to Lorwood incessantly. An open score, even if it's only one in miniature size, makes quite a good screen for a small revolver, and thus screened on the side of the audience, the weapon could have been seen from nowhere else in the hall except from the orchestra, where everybody was supposed to be busy either playing or counting bars. (Mind, I say "supposed": I gave you detailed particulars earlier as to how my suspicions were modified when I had gone over the possibilities with Ransom's help—Ransom's, forsooth!) But all this merely for what it is worth.

You will tell me that Ransom has only a very weak motive. Darling, I know. But the devil of it is that *everybody has only a weak motive.* You will perhaps say, further, that he could not have fired the shot from where he was *and* thrown the revolver in front of Dashwood (another revolver, admittedly), unless possibly he had an accomplice. To which I reply that there *was* an accomplice, not possibly, but certainly, now that we know that two different weapons are involved. At least I shall have the surprise of my life if that is not the case. For why, if you can fling a weapon at a certain spot after firing a shot, should not one and the same weapon perform both actions, if the same person is responsible for them?

Need I add that J. R. is being watched?

Now I proceed to Rookdale to lunch. More later on, dearest. Hug the children for me. I have hardly mentioned them these days, but you know they are in my mind as often as there is the smallest crevice left open for them. You too!

Sunday evening.

Another motive. Letty! This time a strong one, but completely dissociated from opportunity, so far as I can see; unless...but no, I need no longer fetch things quite so far.

First let me tell you about my talk with Humphrey in the downstairs study. After apologising for any appearance of abusing his hospitality and pointing out that I could obviously not have accepted it if I had suspected him, I asked him for an explanation as to how he got to Beatrice so quickly after the shot, seeing that he must have been in the auditorium. He gave it quite frankly, I thought, and it seems to hold water, though it is unfortunately not the only possible explanation. It appears that the Gillighans' seats (remember that Beatrice is usually in the audience, not in the orchestra) are in the front row of the balcony, somewhat to the left. But on the nights Beatrice plays second harp Humphrey does not sit there. He likes to watch her play, he says, as he thinks she is never more beautiful and adorable than when seated at her harp—a very becoming instrument, of course. You know he's had her painted at it by Grinston. Unfortunately it completely unnerves her to know that her husband is watching her and to see him in front of her incessantly staring at her, as he simply can't help doing. It may only be part of her pose in thinking Humphrey unbearable—and whatever adjectives of a similar nature she may use. Anyhow, there it is. So on the nights she is in the orchestra he obediently goes and sits somewhere else, without telling her where, which makes her feel all right. And, cunning brute that he is, he sits anywhere during a work in which she does not play, and then when her turn comes he goes to the side of the balcony, directly opposite Ransom's new and detested seat, sitting right above and behind her, so that he can watch her without her being aware of it and be quite close to her. And that, if he tells the truth, is where he was on the fatal Thursday. There is a gangway and an exit directly behind him and it leads immediately to the top of a short flight of stairs going down to the orchestra exit on the extreme right, just under the end of the balcony. It's only a matter of a dozen steps or so, I remember. You can get to the orchestra, where Beatrice sits so picturesquely at her harp, in a quarter of a minute, I should judge.

That is that. And now for your introduction to Lady Grampian, née Miss Laetitia Parkings, or in brief Letty, as she asked me almost immediately to call her, in her disarmingly friendly and trusting way. Any friend of Beatrice's is *her* friend— you know the kind of thing—and indeed these two sisters are amazingly attached to each other, so much so that one is almost tempted to disbelieve in so close a family relationship, which usually means a kind of affectionate detachment. But then they are extremely unlike each other. Letty has nothing of Beatrice's stately and placid beauty. She is small, very pretty in a slightly wan, shell-pink way; not shy, though, as you would expect from her appearance. Her advances to me (perfectly innocuous, by the way) showed that. And I knew that she must be headstrong, for I remembered that she had obstinately refused to follow up any opportunity for a divorce offered her with such plentiful gener-osity by her husband.

But now listen. She and Beatrice blurted it all out over coffee in that lovely long drawing-room after lunch, where we sat very cosily over a log fire that was more ornamental and comforting than strictly necessary, for the day had only a just perceptible nip in the air, to which was added the faint tang of a bonfire in one of the adjoining gardens—the ideal October day, yet with a hint of approaching gloom.

But I wander. What the two did blurt out, rather to the discomfort of Humphrey, I thought, was that Letty was destined to be hoist with her own petard—literally with a vengeance. For N. G., who really did not at all mind remaining un-re-marriageable, as I think I told you before, found about six month ago that he could now have his own back. Poor Letty, as she confessed quite frankly—simply because she was glad, I think, to talk about it and relieve her feelings, which must be in a pretty tangle just at the moment—fell head over ears in love with another man she had met at the house of friends in London, an air-force officer of romantic and chivalrous leanings that contrasted very favourably with her husband's disposition. He was as keen on her as she on him, and it was she now who wanted a divorce.

Unfortunately, however, she was injudicious enough, instead of eating humble pie by appealing to N. G. for release (in any way he pleased), to put it to him that she would now after all do him the favour of divorcing him. All he need do was to furnish the necessary proofs, of which unfortunately she had none now, and she would see to it as soon as possible. If she had not been a little fool, she would have seen that this would put his back up, as indeed it did. He agreed to meet her in town, gave her a topping lunch at the "Coq-à-l'âne" and pleasantly told her over the meal that he was quite content to go on being her husband. He informed her in the most urbane manner that he would never importune her with any request to live with him again, and as they were therefore both perfectly happy as they were, he saw no reason for any change and for creating an unnecessary scandal.

Thereupon she had, of course, to spill the beans and to confess the reason for her sudden desire for a divorce, which he must have already guessed, and it seemed to give him exquisite pleasure to tell her quietly, in a public place where the most perfect manners had to be outwardly preserved, that he felt it would be an excellent opportunity for her to learn all about life and to acquire some sympathy with human frailty and difficulties if she had to face a little of the adversity she had caused him to suffer. I leave you to imagine her fury, which was of course increased tenfold by her knowledge that he had in fact suffered nothing at all and by his intolerably hypocritical pretence that he was doing her a good turn, when he knew perfectly well that he was ruining her chances of happiness for the second time in her young life. What made matters worse was that the fury had to be suppressed. You are enough of a psychologist to understand that when a victim is given first-rate material for a highly dramatic scene, the aggressor's choice of a place where it cannot possibly be enacted in the manner that befits it, causes high-tension feelings to be bottled up at such an unbearable pressure that sooner or later an explosion of the utmost violence is bound to occur.

I am prepared to believe—in fact I am positively certain— that Letty was emotionally predisposed to go to any length to revenge herself for the peculiarly hideous combination of injury and insult inflicted on her by her scamp of a husband. I must warn you, darling, that I am merely theorising, though I have said that so often that I can hardly doubt your being perfectly well aware of it. If I reiterate it tiresomely, I hope you will understand that I am impelled to do so merely because this happens to be a case of friends and that I feel rather guilty—unless I should happen to find *them* to be—at speculating about them in this manner. I am really trying to assure myself, rather than you, that I am simply considering outside possibilities, and fortunately I am quite able to persuade myself that I do not actually go so far as to formulate any definite suspicions.

All the same, this has roused me, and what I am going to do this very night, however long it may take me, is to go through all my material (of which you have copies) and all my notes (which are brief précis of my all too long and diffuse letters to you) and to see if I cannot get at some sort of co-ordination of facts that will give me a definite lead.

I have certain ideas, of course, and I think I am pretty sure about a large number of definite eliminations. The residue is still amazingly confusing, all the same, owing to the bewildering number of possibilities and motives, and the fact that the latter are all insufficiently strong on the face of it does not simplify my problem. Or does it, perhaps? Yes, just possibly. For I am more and more inclined to think that if no motive was strong enough, then I must look for some unusual temperamental disposition, some eccentricity, some warped emotional state, even lunacy, perhaps. And look for that I shall, forthwith. Also, since material clues seem to avail little or nothing, although I have of course borne them constantly in mind and shall go on doing so, I have to rely once again on psychology, at the risk of earning another scornful observation from old Higgy about my getting at a solution in a roundabout way when it could have been reached by the aid of common sense alone—though he never tells me how. Well, or perhaps with the hope of converting him at last. One never knows.

But then I doubt if psychology, plus possible clues, will do the trick by themselves this time. You see, I am still haunted by the notion that some purely musical point is escaping me. Ransom gave me much valuable help by drawing my attention to certain probabilities and improbabilities with the aid of Strauss's score, which is not merely all Greek (I do at least remember the Greek alphabet) but Egyptian hieroglyphs to me; and though you may have generously forgotten it, you too gave me a valuable lead that could not possibly have occurred to me by pointing out Ransom's remark that in Strauss any one of a number of instruments might cease to play for a moment without anybody's being the wiser, so far as hearing is concerned. Seeing, of course, is another matter; but nobody saw anything, utterly incredible as it seems.

I forgot to tell you, by the way, that we advertised for any one who had been in the audience on the 29th, and who had anything whatever of interest to tell us as an eye-witness, to come forward and write to me. But although I got innumerable crazy letters (not worth bothering you with) and interviewed several of the more promising writers, I got absolutely nothing but the kind of confusion that arises when people are wise after the event and want to show off. They all persuaded themselves that what they had to say was of immense interest and value, but it all amounted to vague impressions at the best and to sheer imagination or even deliberate invention at the worst. Of course there were indignant letters to the papers to the effect that the Police, though put in possession by the writers of the most valuable and suggestive information, was doing nothing, and what was justice in this country coming to, and so forth. All quite footling.

Now I *must* set to work, dearest. I shall first of all read those articles of J. R.'s again where he discusses Strauss and where he theorises about the murder. You got me something from that; I may get more. I'll write to-morrow if I have come to any conclusions worth mentioning.

Ever most attachedly yours,

ALAN.

Monday, 17th October

4 G.S,
M'POOL.

17. X. 38.

DEAREST,

What a night! I've been at it from 11.30, when I went across
the square to post my budget to you, until nearly 4 this morning.
But of course the indefatigable D. I. Hope was astir again by 9
o'clock. What a Hope!

Well, I think I am on to something. Possess your soul in
patience, for I can't possibly show any results until this evening,
if it please the powers above that I may do so then. Meanwhile I
shall have a hell of a day taking "certain measures," as they say in
the detective classics and in the House of Commons at times of
national crisis. The essence is secrecy, here as there. But I trust I
may report to you in full to-morrow, in which case you may raise
your hands in horrified astonishment. I must say I rather dread
the outcome, if my conjectures, which are really little more than
a sort of intuitive apprehension so far, are right; for it won't be
at all the laying of an out-and-out villain by the heels. There are
times when I loathe my job. If only it weren't so fascinatingly
interesting!

I haven't much time now, darling, but I'll just allay your
possibly uncomfortable suspicions a little. Mind you, I have
not definitely discarded either the Ransom claim or the

Letty-Beatrice-Humphrey complex. I have shown you how difficult it is to believe, not only in Ransom's motive, but in the possibility of two weapons being involved if he were the culprit. As for the Grampian-Gillighan group, whom I have *not* exonerated even unconsciously because they are friends, I simply disbelieve in their guilt, as indeed in Ransom's, chiefly because I can now much more readily believe in someone else's. Against that I may still urge that Beatrice would go to the limit in doing deeds of the utmost heroism or the utmost villainy for her dear little sister, I do believe, and you will not find it difficult to agree that doting Humphrey, if it came to serving Beatrice, would in turn be *capable de tout*.

I have also considered whether Letty, who could not possibly have done the foul deed (or the noble one, as the perpetrator is sure to think) herself, because we know that she was at Harmsford that night, might have had some sort of understanding with, possibly even some hold over, one of the members of the orchestra. Well, if I thought so, I should naturally think first of all of those who had been in the orchestra at Harmsford under Grampian, and whom Letty may have known, though that is not very likely. They were, according to their own account in their letters to me: Cohen, one of the cellists, Tufton, the first bassoon, and Dipton, the timpanist. Of these the last is the most unlikely because he was placed too high up, we think. There is also Evans, the pathetic-comic first clarinet, who had *not* told me that he had been at Harmsford and from whom I extorted the information at my interview with him. He is the most suspicious, if there is anything in this at all. But all these four people came to M'pool at N. G.'s recommendation, because he remembered them as good players, and since M'pool as against H'ford meant promotion, they had no reason to feel murderous about him, at any rate on that score.

But how about this? You remember Ailner's report about Councillor Rossingham of Harmsford? I was in too much of a hurry about getting on with my notes yesterday to remember to tell you that I had a detailed account of N. G.'s goings-on at "England's Healthiest Resort," as the posters have it, at the Gillighans' yesterday. Letty was by no means backward about airing her former grievances, which have by this time become a source of mere mild excitement and amusement, since they can no longer affect her feelings or interfere with her impending happiness; and as the matter is apparently common gossip at H., I can now tell you a thing I had at once read between the lines of Ailner's confidences, a thing he may or may not have surmised (you did, you remember). The weekend girl who had been the direct cause of Letty's retirement from N. G.'s bed and board was, I may as well say "of course," Mr. Rossingham's own daughter, a fact which for obvious reasons he had not thought it desirable to disclose to our upright Ailner, though I have no doubt he would have done so if it had been strictly necessary, which it wasn't.

Well, Mr. Rossingham is a very rich man, a gentleman, Letty tells us, not in the least disposed to let anybody get the better of him, and he was in particularly close touch with the orchestra personnel, as he was the member of the Committee who had taken it upon himself to keep in touch with the players and to do what he could to look after their personal welfare. As a hard-headed business man, he was just the person to see that shiftless musicians were not in any way imposed on by landlords and others; he enjoyed organising and bossing and showing all round a great deal of benevolence and helpfulness that did not cost him anything but a certain amount of his leisure, with which he hardly knew what to do. Several members of the H'ford orchestra were under considerable obligations to him in one way or another. Make what you will of that, O astute one.

As to Evans, I felt that he came into the picture a little for another reason, I am bound to say. I told you yesterday that I was inclined to look for some oddity of character, and Evans, as you will understand from the note I made on his letter, was my first and most obvious choice. But the very obviousness of that choice led me on to look for something less evident and more subtle. Appearances are so deceptive once one gets on the psychological tack. But there's no need to tell you where my further conclusions are leading me, until I know that my instinct is right. Instinct! Oh, Higgy, if you but knew!

And now, my darling, I am going to see a lady. No, not Beatrice, nor Miss Jarvis. Nothing so semi-angelic as a harp player—and these two really must look, when seated at their instruments, as though they were rehearsing for the life to come. To allay your apprehensions, I will say that the object of my attention to-day is no other than Mrs. Horsfall. And to Barrows Row, or rather the back thereof, I am now impatient to bend my steps.

I'll leave this open for a possible note I may want to add before I post it.

Ever yours,

ALAN.

6 p.m.

No, nothing more for the moment, except that I am going to the Hippodrome, first house, 6.20, for a little relaxation—if that's what they call it. So long, then, dear. I may write again to-night, but I hope not. I hope to be too busy later in the evening.

Tuesday, 18th October

MY DEAREST JULIA,

The best hotel note-paper, instead of the scraps I've been sending you, indicates that I am elated. I am also in a rather solemn frame of mind. The former because I was right, and it's all over (but I can't come home yet until it's all cleared up, inquest and all: that's why I'm writing this, for you'll be dying of curiosity); the latter because—well, as I thought, I utterly fail to enjoy laying the murderer by the heels and can feel no sort of satisfaction at having carried out justice that is indeed blind. The only thing that can make me feel at all like wanting to remain in its service is that I was able to take it upon myself to modify its idiotic procedure (for complete impartiality, admirable as a principle, can also be on occasion as wicked as any crime you like to think of)—to modify its procedure to a sufficiently great extent to give its victim—for I insist that he was that quite as much as N. G. himself—the chance, not to escape it, of course, but to make his own choice of his punishment.

Lovelock, my dear, is dead. He threw himself out of his bed-sitting-room window on the second floor, which at the back of the house, where it is, actually becomes the third floor, as there is a yard leading straight out of a basement, the house standing on a slope shelving down to one of the canals you keep coming upon at odd and unexpected corners of this town, always in rather slummy and depressing districts. I don't know why Lovelock lived in this rather miserable way; probably because he had never known anything better and was unaware that it *was* miserable, particularly. He was the sort that would not have been happier anywhere else.

He did what I hoped he would do in some way; I could not, of course, imagine, much less suggest, how. But I think he understood; anyhow, he had thanked me in a curious, solemn sort of way for my kindness, which had not really amounted to anything, and my manner had been stern, the more so because I felt quite otherwise and could not trust myself to be sympathetic. It simply amounted to this: when he knew that he was found out, I promised, as a purely personal matter, that he should not be arrested until this morning, provided he did not make any attempt at getting away. I admit I should have liked him to escape, but needless to say there was no question of that, and I had to assure him that there was no possible chance, as the Police had strict orders to watch him closely. I saw him home myself, not unaccompanied by invisible plain-clothes men, but told him that he would be left alone for the night so long as he kept inside the house. The front was watched, and so was even the tow-path that runs alongside the canal outside the wall of the backyard. The sides of the yard are cut off by the side-walls of two tall houses that go right down to the tow-path, both windowless. So there was no way out. But there was a way out of life altogether, and I am glad he took it. It can't have hurt him more than being alive did.

But I am telling it all backwards. You want to know what made me make for this very inconspicuous fellow at all. Well, in the first place perhaps his inconspicuousness. I can't quite tell. But I'd had an uneasy feeling about him, I suppose ever since I got his letter, unaware as I was of it myself at the time. You see, when it came to going through all the stuff again on Sunday night, I could not help being struck by the fact that of all the writers (and I assure you that includes those whose letters I did not bother you with) Lovelock was the only one who did not refer to the murder at all, and to N. G. only quite casually. Not that there would have been much in this by itself, but in conjunction with other things that cropped up I did feel—rather than think—this to be of some significance.

Now these other things would not, I daresay, have fixed themselves in my mind if I had not, for the moment at any rate, discarded all other theories and suspicions in order to concentrate on this very unobtrusive man Lovelock. Anyhow, I decided to read the evidence, if my notes and the newspaper cuttings could be called that by any stretch of the imagination, in the light of Lovelock's then purely hypothetical guilt. And what did I find quite early in my search? You remember, dear, that I said I wanted to give Ransom's articles my attention again because I felt that there might be some technical point in them I had, in my ignorance of music, overlooked, one very useful point of that kind having already arisen from the articles earlier, thanks to you.

Will you turn back to the cutting of J. R.'s article on Strauss's "Heldenleben," dated Sept. 26, which I sent you about ten days ago? You will see there, in the last paragraph but one, that at one of the rehearsals from which J. R. was afterwards excluded to his considerable annoyance (though he pretended not to mind), the fourth oboist was allowed by N. G. to drop out of his part "before he came to a break where he changes over to the cor anglais, in order to save his breath for a part that stands out prominently in the latter instrument." Well, even I, with the help of one of the staff at the Public Library, could see from the score (I promptly borrowed one from there, not wanting to drag J. R. in again) that before that cor anglais entry the four oboes all play the same thing together (could you call it "in unison"?), and that obviously it can make no material difference to the music if one drops out and only three play on. And the only passage where such a change happens in just this way, we found, occurs round about our famous cue number 79.

Very well. And what happens, I asked myself, when an oboe player changes over to the cor anglais? Again even I can tell, for I've seen it done; from which you may gather that there is after all something to be said for people who go to watch an orchestra with their eyes rather than to attend to it with their ears. Or is that special pleading? Anyhow, I did know that the player keeps the instrument he is not using for the moment beside him on the floor and that he bends down to make the change, disappearing, if you like to make it graphic and in this case suggestive, partly behind the music on his desk. This was better, you'll admit, and I couldn't help seeing, than Ransom burying his head in a miniature score, which is very much smaller than an orchestral part.

Now if you look up the lists of the orchestra Ransom and I had compiled and marked according to our analysis of their candidature for the murdership (how I enrich the English language!), you will find that on the first one the cor anglais (4th oboe) appears as entirely above suspicion, simply because we thought he must have been playing. On the second, revised list we mark him still as engaged in playing, but possible as a murderer, without regarding him as suspicious, or even doubtful; whereas I now concluded that he had in fact a first-class opportunity.

So much for that. But what about motive?, I was bound to ask myself. Could he have had a strong enough grudge against N. G. to want to kill him? If so, I felt it would not be, as in the case of Dashwood or Gough, for instance, a musician's grudge. If it had been that, I am pretty sure something of it would have come out in his letter to me. On the other hand, if the thing was personal, that would account, in the case of a rather unhappily repressed person like him, for a deliberate suppression of any sort of direct allusion to his attitude towards the conductor. But how had I formed the impression that he was repressed? I had not been told, yet somehow I was aware of it. I had not seen him at all, I ought to mention. That impression, then, can only have come from something I was told, and on looking at my notes I found my memory of two things returning.

One was that Miss Jarvis had befriended him in a kindly, rather patronising way, and of course only when it suited her and she was not particularly keen on attracting any of the busier bees to her honey-pot fragrance at the moment. But he must have felt her patronage, for these unhappily self-conscious people are inordinately sensitive, and no doubt it only aggravated his inferiority complex. We may be sure he was thoroughly miserable about Gwenny, and since she must have quite noticeably treated him with condescension and capriciously, I felt sure that he would not have exposed himself to being made ridiculous by her had he not been desperately in love with her and quite unable to keep away from her, in spite of the fact that he must have known his case to be hopeless.

My next deduction was—and I don't pride myself on any subtlety here, for it all seems quite evident to me—that a man who is hopelessly in love with a girl, an unprepossessing man who feels himself her inferior, must be all the time desperately watching for any signs of attention to other men on her part, and still more of advances of other men to her. He will, unless he has the strength to give up all thoughts of her, live in a state of seething ferment, if he is compelled to be as constantly near the girl as Lovelock was to Gwenny, and nurse within himself a state of furious jealousy every time he sees another fellow talk to her, let alone take her out to lunch, as he must have seen several of his colleagues do time after time. And these jealous lovers find out all sorts of things, sometimes indeed things that don't happen at all. He must have known perfectly well that she did not look with disfavour upon Dashwood, whom he knew to be a married man, and that may have seemed to him a sure sign that she was going to get herself into some extremely unpleasant trouble. As for Grampian, with his unsavoury reputation, taking her into the Langdon grill, a place he himself could not have aspired to in his wildest dreams, it must have seemed to him like an express journey to perdition.

Here was motive enough, if you like, both for the murder of N. G. and the implication of Dashwood. Could both be accomplished at one fell swoop? I could hardly doubt any longer that he must at least have asked himself that question a hundred times. If, that is, he really was in love with Gwenny. I had no definite confirmation of that, only a "hunch." Then it came to me that Mrs. Horsfall had overheard N. G. asking Gwenny to lunch, of course not in public, for she alone was there, having a word *with Mr. Lovelock*. I had really quite forgotten that, and had not even kept a note of it, so casual and unimportant had it seemed; but it is odd how things begin to start up again in your mind in a certain context, though they have been relegated as useless to its farthest recesses.

Which brings me at last to the reason for my second visit to Mrs. H. She professed to be very pleased to see me, she was sure, and it took me hardly more time than I shall spend writing it to bring her round to the subject of Mr. Lovelock's devotion to Miss Jarvis, in such a way that she felt quite sure that she herself had brought up the subject. In love with Miss Jarvis?! Goodness her! She should just think so. To start with, everybody was. But that Mr. Lovelock, well, he was just barmy about her, as she had only told her husband the other day. "*Love*lock" was right! Yes, she had told her Harry how Mr. Lovelock was always hanging round, though he got little enough chance, poor little chap, and how he had found out that Miss Jarvis always turned up early on rehearsal days, twenty minutes or half an hour sometimes, because she wanted to tune her harp before they started. Why a harp should take so long to tune was more than she could tell, but Miss Jarvis, who always had a nice word to say to her if she was cleaning anywhere near her, had told her that it was a funny instrument, directly you had played on a string it was almost out of tune again; whereupon she, Mrs. H., had observed that well, her dear, if she got as much money for tuning as she did for playing, she'd do well enough.

And then Mr. Lovelock had turned up, much too early, and of course any fool could see why. But he had been put out, somehow, perhaps not expecting to find a duenna with a mop and duster, and had then perversely taken no notice at all of Miss Jarvis, but turned all his attention to Mrs. H. and begun to chaff her something chronic. He was funny that way, and could sometimes make people laugh like anything; well, of course, he had been on the halls, a sort of clown or something. Anyway, he had asked her to stand up on the rostrum, in Sir Noel's place, and pretend she was the conductor, and said he'd bet she could do just as well, and she believed it, for anybody could wag a stick about in the air, and why anybody should be knighted for that was more than she could see. Anyhow, she started waving her duster in the air as if she was Sir Noel himself in all his glory, and she and Miss Jarvis had laughed fit to bust theìrselves. But there, Mr. Lovelock *was* a queer one, for by that time he'd stopped taking any notice of her and was fiddling about with his pipe (forgive her uncertain musical terminology, as you would forgive mine!), mending it or something.

That was all, I think, apart from trimmings and garnishings that would have shamed *a filet de bœuf à la jardinière*. It was quite enough in all conscience. Just think. Or can't you? Are you too utterly bewildered? Well, it fairly stunned me for a bit, the way things concentrated themselves on this poor wretch Lovelock— for I knew him to be that by this time, before I had set eyes on him. A sort of clown! Been on the halls! Of course I looked at his letter again when I got back, and there it was, sure enough. Only, like a fool, I hadn't seen it. Or perhaps that was natural enough. Perhaps, indeed, I was not meant to see it. For look at his letter. He says: "I used to be at music halls before I joined the M'pool Orch." Read in conjunction with what had gone before, namely the information that he played oboe at the Hippodrome, this could only be taken to mean that he had always played in music-hall orchestras. Was he deliberately drawing my attention away from his having been *on the music-hall stage*? I don't know even now, but seen in the light of what followed, it looks more than likely.

Can you wonder that I wanted to go to the Hippodrome? Ah, you have misjudged me, my Julia: I did not go frivolously when I had work to do. It *was* my work. But I still had time to do a great deal of spade-work, for I had seen Mrs. Horsfall before lunch. First of all I went through my papers once more: it is always a good thing to do that when a crop of new facts has emerged, for one may easily find that some apparently insignificant fact suddenly shows quite a new face. And what did I find? Gough too, in his letter, said that he played at a music-hall, and I found on inquiring at the hotel office downstairs that the only music-hall left in M'pool, in these degenerate days of cinemas, is the Hippodrome.

That was not all, by any means. Did you look at the addresses at the head of all those letters from the orchestra of which I sent you copies? Perhaps. But did you take them in? Almost certainly not. Why should you? And, come to that, why should I have? Although I can't persuade myself, unfortunately, that I have not grossly neglected my duty in failing to notice all these addresses, and perhaps even following them up by going to see all these diggings, I do plead on my own behalf that unless one has some special reason for doing so, one simply does not attach any significance to addresses in the first place. Doubtless this is a weak defence, but I can at least say that in the second place it did occur to me that I might just possibly find something there. Well, not having memorised all those addresses, even if I did give them a momentary attention, I had not noticed that the house at Birchton (a suburb of jerry-built sham-Tudor) from which Gough wrote is, believe it or not, the one at which I had visited the Mystic Trumpeter, Mr. Holborne!

This sent me back to the Civic Hall, for I felt by this time that I owed it to the Spirit of the Yard, as embodied by Higgy, to find, if possible, a material clue or two in addition to my accumulating collection of abstruse musical and psychological points. I knew where to look now, though I am bound to say that without those m. and p. points I should have found it a much harder and certainly longer job to interpret the exact meaning of clues. That is to say, although I could not have failed to find them, they would not have pointed with any certainty to a solution of the crime. I could not have applied them to any particular person. That is indeed why I paid no detailed attention to the "dungeon" for so long and took no notice, I'm afraid, when you asked me about it. But I always knew that it was likely to become a vital factor, in my own good time.

And now for the *scène à faire*. I went to the Hippodrome with Inspector Masterman, one of the best of the locals. (Plain clothes, of course.) We went, as I think I told you, to the "first house," at 6.20, simply because I hoped to get things over early; but as it happened this proved a considerable help. You see, it was Monday, and therefore a new show, and the orchestra—or those who sit far enough in front to be able to see the stage— make a point of seeing as much as they can of what is going on on the stage, whenever they are not actually playing. They have had only perfunctory and incomplete rehearsals, and the later shows, of course, they no longer watch. Masterman and I occupied the proscenium box on the prompt side, purposely, because I had found out that I could watch the oboe player easily from there, and I knew that he would not notice us with the house lights turned down, even while he was not playing, apart from which, you remember, he did not know me by sight, much less my colleague.

I had looked for nothing beyond a simple view of him, which would have been interesting enough, I assure you. There he was, much as I had expected him to be. Very short, almost dwarfish, yet without the attraction of frailty and delicacy that makes small men interesting to some women. He was rather fleshy, in a puffy and pasty sort of way, yet gave the impression of weakness and even of cowardice, not of the physical kind, for he looked as though he cared little what happened to his body, but in the face of people who dominate by success or by character. One of the downtrodden right enough, yet with something in his face that was, if not noble, at any rate not slavish. One could easily imagine him feeling fiercely rebellious, yet unable to act openly on his subversive impulses. I daresay I was influenced in my judgment by preconceptions to a certain extent, but I can't help feeling sure that even if I had known nothing of his history, I could not have failed to see that here was the face of a man who is accustomed to show himself to the world as something he is not, but does it with a continual sensation of hidden, smouldering protest. "A clown or something." Even Mrs. Horsfall had seen it (you see, she did not *know* whether he had been a clown). Yes, the face of a tragic clown. Pagliaccio. He who gets slapped.

But I was in luck by this time. I shudder at calling it that, but professionally speaking it is true. For I found that presently he did begin to watch the turns, and could do so easily enough, as he sat in the front row, immediately behind the little curtained railing that separates the orchestra from the stalls, to the left of the conductor and therefore facing us. To the first two or three numbers he paid little attention, even when he was not busy playing, as little as I, and much less than I paid to him. But then came a surprising *volte-face*. The turn was, my programme reminds me, "Les Infallibles (this is music-hall French), Continental and Trans-Atlantic Aiming Act." No, darling, it does not mean that these two smart young fellows, fancifully attired in purple dinner-jackets with orange shirts and green ties, shoot right from France (if that is their home) to America; but they do some quite remarkable tricks, so far as I could spare attention to see, one with darts and the other with pistols. They end by standing with their heads in front of each other's targets and potting at each other right and left about an inch from each ear (on the outside).

What interested me, however, was the extraordinary passion with which Lovelock suddenly began to follow this performance. I saw him tap Gough on the shoulder and draw his attention to the turn, but apparently not so much to ask him to admire it as to show a sort of half-envious and half-superior contempt for it. I could see him shrugging his shoulders, as though accompanying some such remark as "That's easy" or "That's been done before"; and what struck me next was that he reserved his criticism for the pistol-shooter alone, passing the dart-thrower's performance without any particular interest as, let us say, "all right in its way."

After that he lost interest again in the next two items. But once more I was struck during the following one by an amazing change, not only from his detachment, but from the attitude he had assumed towards the alleged "infallibles." The turn was now that of a couple who each in turn sang sentimental ditties. They had their own accompanist at the piano, so that the orchestra was idle, at any rate until at the very end it was urged by an oily, inviting gesture from the conductor to join in the last verse of a duet in a final burst of glory. It was during the earlier stages of this duet that Masterman and I became more than ever interested in Lovelock. The piece exploited the music-hall public's ineradicable delight in slushy pathos. The young man, who had been saucy enough a minute before, suddenly became gawky, sickly and helpless, while the girl, who had archly and artfully glossed over the first signs of decaying bloom by a ribbon tied into a colossal bow in her hair, redoubled her sauce. She was not unattractive to anyone less spoilt than I, as I am sure Lovelock was, poor chap. She certainly appealed to something in him, in a way, I could see, and when I heard the refrain of the duet, an inane and sloppy piece, yet with something of human truth about it that was quite well suggested by the two in a slick, theatrical sort of way, I could see just where it hit him. For the words of that refrain, which I noted in my programme, were as follows:

She: I've had lovers galore,
   And I mean to have more;
      So I tell you, my lad,
      I'll be ever so glad,
   If you'll hop it and leave me alone.

He: Girls like you, I'm aware,
   Love but glamour and glare;
      But although you are bad,
      P'raps one day you'll be glad,
   When you're old, to at last be my own.

Or something very like it. I can't be sure of every word, but will guarantee the split infinitive, if it's any comfort to you.

Well, Lovelock's reaction to this miniature tragedy of a jilted goof visibly had the effect of awakening echoes of a poignantly personal feeling in him. His face worked spasmodically and I could see that this cheap imitation of his own plight cut him to the quick. He was not enough of an artist to see the cheapness, but felt its application to his own case, so unexpectedly sprung on him, acutely. So much so that when the comparatively happy ending came, with its idiotic promise of long-deferred bliss:

> He: ⎫
> She: ⎬ When we're old, to at last be   my / your   own!

he had so far forgotten himself as to fail to join at once in the aforesaid orchestral burst. It was as though he had to be roused violently out of a painful dream.

After that he showed no further concern in the performance, except of course that he continued to play whenever required. For me, Poirot... I mean, as for me, Hope, I was quite unable to attend further either to the music or the hall. Not only did I have far too much to think about, and to think quickly, but twice in the course of the performance I had to hold little receptions at the back of our box, of the excellent officers Masterman had sent out into the town, who were now returning with their reports and with some trophies that both gladdened and saddened my heart, the one professionally, the other humanly. However, the profession was uppermost now, and the job had to be cleaned up.

The next thing, or rather it was a simultaneous thing, for the officer who had come in first carried it out while I was dealing with the second one, was to discover where we could conveniently get hold of Lovelock, and if possible of Gough too, though that was less urgent and it was enough to know that he was being adequately watched. Fortunately we learnt from the stagedoor-keeper that between the first and the second house, when an interval of thirty minutes occurs, the members of the orchestra, not having time to get home or even to their rather dismal club, get themselves a drink and a snack at one of the numerous surrounding pubs; and more fortunately still he knew that Mr. Lovelock and Mr. Gough invariably frequented the Gorgon's Head over the way. We watched them, of course, but found that they duly repaired thither. Masterman and I followed in, making for two stools at the bar next to them, engaged in a heated discussion of the dart and pistol feats performed by the "infallibles." Masterman opined that the pistol-shooter was the cleverer of the two, whereas I stoutly maintained that I had thought far more of the dart-thrower and regarded the shooter as a bit of a fraud, who had really made things quite easy for himself while cleverly pretending that they were difficult. He had, after all, done nothing any normally good marksman would have been unable to do. He had not, for instance, fired any shots with his head upside down aiming backwards through his straddled legs—or whatever it was I invented on the spur of the moment.

Lovelock, who was next to me, could not help listening to all this and, as I had expected, he looked so deeply interested that I could easily venture to address him, having already, so to speak, talked at him, thus drawing him almost imperceptibly into the conversation.

"Don't you agree, Mr. er…um…," I said, "that this man was no great shakes? I saw you in the orchestra, you know, and you looked to me as if you might know something about music-hall turns."

That fetched him, of course.

"Know something, sir? I should think I do know something. I was on the halls myself for a good many years, ever since I was a kid, working with my dad."

"What was it you did, may I ask?" I did ask.

"Oh well, a bit of everything: conjuring, tumbling, musical stunts, trick…well, things like that, you know."

"But you stopped yourself just now," I put in quickly, before he had got over the curious hesitation and slight confusion that had come over him. "Trick what, were you going to say?"

"Oh, nothing, sir; I told you: conjuring tricks."

"You weren't going to say trick shooting, by any chance, were you, Mr. Lovelock?"

At that his jaw fell, and I am afraid—no, I don't mean that: I am glad to say—a sickening qualm came over me; for it wasn't pleasant to see that look of terror come into his eyes so suddenly, the look of the moral weakling who is accustomed to being out-witted or bullied and has never learnt to cultivate the presence of mind that lets people wriggle out of small verbal entanglements. For people like Lovelock these entanglements, which ought to be ridden over roughshod with an overwhelming avalanche of talk, at once mean a trap from which there is no escape. There was none for him, and it was quite as much the discovery that I knew his name as my hitting plumb into the middle of his secret that made him drop all his defences at once.

There was nobody at the bar but ourselves. Our men outside had seen to that, and I had at the very first handed one of my cards to the barmaid, asking her to join her boss, to whom in turn I had scribbled a request to detain her behind the scenes and to place a private room at our disposal immediately, but not to come into the bar until I rang the bell. This I now did, and mine host at once appeared with a polite and at the same time rather apprehensive and inquisitive "This way, gentlemen." Having informed Lovelock and Gough who we were, I asked the former to come into the adjoining small parlour with me, while Masterman took charge of Gough, and there told him that the Police had gone to his lodgings with a search-warrant and found quite a little assortment of very odd-looking firearms under a loose floorboard, while extra cartridges fitting Prof. Gillighan's revolver had been discovered at the house where Gough was lodging, not indeed in his room, but in the custody of Mr. Holborne, who was already under arrest.

Lovelock was miserably speechless. Gough, on the other hand, Masterman told me later, became only too voluble for a minute or so. His chief object, apart from professing his own innocence and utter ignorance of the cartridges at Dilling Street, seemed to be to take a last opportunity of incriminating Dashwood, whom, he said, Holborne told him he had actually seen in the act of abstracting the revolver from Humphrey's desk. Whether this was true or not I don't know, and it doesn't matter, for Masterman disposed of it by telling Gough that we already knew of Dashwood's petty larceny by his own confession and were perfectly satisfied, nevertheless, that he had not committed the murder.

Meanwhile I proposed to tell Lovelock exactly how that murder had been committed, asking him to stop me if he found me wrong anywhere. He did not; he merely listened, utterly crushed and flabbergasted.

It was like this: Lovelock and Gough hobnobbed nightly together at the Gorgon's Head and, as the former confirmed, sometimes after the second Hippodrome performance at his room in Allport Street, which is a quarter of an hour's walk from the theatre, according to my subsequent discovery, and on Gough's way to Birchton. They had often aired their grievances against Grampian to each other, ever since he first came to M'pool, and their hatred of him had come to a head, Gough's on account of his dismissal, for which he neatly swept Dashwood as well into the orbit of his detestation, and Lovelock's because of his supposed, or possibly real and certainly intended, goings-on with Gwenny Jarvis.

Nothing of this was denied or contradicted. Neither was my suggestion that Lovelock might one night have said something to the effect that he would like to shoot the b...lighter, darling, and had shown Gough his old shooting-trick paraphernalia, which he had kept quite illegally, since it amounted in effect to regular deadly firearms, but I feel sure in all innocent ignorance of thus committing an offence. (All this may not have been quite accurate, but he let it pass.)

Then, providentially, if the Devil has a share in providence,

Gough found Humphrey's revolver in the cloakroom at the Civic Hall and told Lovelock about it after he had first secured it at his diggings. A plan then began to mature between the two, for it obviously removed a big obstacle for Lovelock, who could not very well trust himself with firing the revolver undetected as well as chucking it some distance away in front of Dashwood with perfect safety. But this was an essential part of the plan for him as well as for Gough. So Gough volunteered to do the chucking, if only he could feel safe about doing so in front of a hall full of people.

I interposed a question here. Why was the murder not planned for a rehearsal, when the danger of having about 2,000 possible witnesses would not arise? But Lovelock explained that, although Gough had favoured that plan, he had dissuaded him from it. They had then agreed that if the risk was worth taking at all, they might as well do the thing in the grand, spectacular style (he did not use these words himself), and moreover—which weighed a good deal more in favour of the actual performance—every orchestral player knew that the attention of people rehearsing is not nearly so keenly concentrated on their work as that of an orchestra in the full swing and excitement of a performance, when one was strung up to the utmost and incapable of noticing anything outside one's share in the music, especially in a work so absorbing and so difficult to play as the Strauss.

Remember that Lovelock had not only been a trick shooter, but also a conjurer, and that a conjurer's skill consists mainly in his ability to judge when the attention of an audience is sufficiently engaged elsewhere for him to perform certain sleights of hand with the certainty of their remaining undetected, even if they are done quite openly. And if the audience at the Civic

Hall was not going to notice anything—which I suggested he was counting on and he said he was absolutely sure of—obviously the orchestra, very busy just then, would know even less that anything queer was going on.

Besides, we have seen that just before the shot was fired Lovelock had left off playing in unison with the other three oboes (by Grampian's special permission, ironically enough) and bent down to change his instruments. It was while he was doing this, half hidden behind his music-desk, that he fired the shot, and he was able to do this while he was bent double and had his face actually turned away from N. G., sideways towards the back of his chair. He was a trick shooter, you see, and could do this sort of thing, almost literally, standing on his head. I knew, as a matter of fact, before it was confirmed by the finding of his weapons, among which was one of the same calibre as Humphrey's, that there must have been a little mirror fixed to it, of the kind used by trick shooters who amaze their audiences by hitting a target on which they have turned their back; because, you see, he had asked Mrs. Horsfall to stand up on N. G.'s rostrum and was bending down "fiddling with his pipe" while she was doing so, all of which seemed to me excessively odd. If he had asked Mrs. H. to conduct with her duster merely for the fun of it, he would certainly have watched her, not turned his attention to something else. That something else, of course, was the trick pistol, which he was enabled by the presence of Mrs. H. to adjust so that he could see N. G. in the little mirror without fail.

People of his sort, he told me with a certain defiant pride, are absolutely sure of themselves, once they have got their gadgets right, and when I asked him whether he had not feared that the shot might go wide and hit somebody in the audience, he said almost indignantly that such a thing had never even occurred to him. These things just don't happen, it seems; and when you come to think of it, rope-walkers of the old-fashioned sort, who used to cross streets from one roof to another without any safe-guard whatever, had that sort of assurance, and they could never have started a career involving such feats, let alone pursued it, if they had not set out with the conviction that accidents simply don't happen. That is how Lovelock worked, as I had indeed con-cluded for myself once I knew he had been a music-hall artist.

When I asked if he had considered the possibility of being searched on the platform, with the rest of the orchestra, he said he had thought this very unlikely, as Humphrey's revolver would be picked up from the platform and naturally taken to be the offending weapon. Still, he was prepared to wipe the fingerprints off his own weapon inside his pocket and drop it through one of the holes into the dungeon. He was pretty sure of being able to do this in case of need, and he did indeed place himself next to the hole nearest his seat when the whole orchestra had jumped up and scattered in confusion all over the platform after the shot. But he said he was really more or less indifferent about its all coming off without a hitch. You see, he was merely taking his revenge on life; he had nothing to gain.

Gough was willing to help, partly from a certain attachment to Lovelock, but much more because he could not resist the chance of dragging Dashwood into the case. His share was easy enough, once Lovelock had convinced him, by some such argu-ment as I have just treated you to, that it was impossible that he should be seen to throw the revolver. All he had to do was to wait until N. G. had fallen and then to take the revolver out of the side pocket of his dinner-jacket (only the leader wears tails in the orchestra) and in the general confusion drop it in front of Dashwood's desk. It was dead easy, for it was natural for the viola players, in front of whom N. G. was bound to fall, to rush forward to go to his assistance. Gough simply rushed with the others and dropped the revolver in the appointed place as he passed. Nobody was looking: all eyes were on the corpse.

But there was a snag, and this is where I saw that Holborne was in it, especially when I had found that Gough was his lodger. It was all neatly and simply planned (so I found from what Lovelock confessed; but I can't always go specifying what I actually discovered for myself—quite a respectable deal, I assure you—and what I had afterwards to drag out of him by way of confirmation or additional information), when it occurred to them that it was no earthly good chucking the revolver in front of Dashwood if it was going to be quite obvious to the most beef-witted of policemen that no shot had been fired from it quite recently. They might have fired one shot at any time, of course, but they knew, or Lovelock at least did, that a gun from which a shot has just been fired is warm and smells. So what?

Gough, as I had conjectured, discussed the matter with Holborne, one of the three trumpeters who had to go under the platform during the "Battle" episode, who eventually declared himself willing to help. I knew of no special grudge he had against N. G., apart from his dismissal, but have now found that he had been treated particularly poisonously over a summer engagement at Harmsford which N. G. had wrecked, such things being subject to the musical director's approval, not because he wanted to queer Holborne's pitch, but simply for the petty and therefore still more infuriating reason that he wished to annoy the Harmsford Orchestra Committee, including his illegitimate father-in-law, so to speak, Councillor Rossingham.

Well, Holborne agreed to fire the revolver off in the dungeon, while the three trumpeters were preparing to play their far-off fanfare through those holes behind the violas; and fortunately, I learnt afterwards, he was able to profit by a little joke he and his colleagues had devised, which was that of nipping quickly into the orchestra green-room and there taking a hasty swig at a bottle of beer brought in for the purpose before they dived in under the orchestra. Holborne, however, had declared that he was feeling rather bilious and would be better without that drink, but would see the boys in a minute when they joined him in the dungeon—or some such cajolery. So he had a minute or two to spare, as according to the score the trumpets can come off the platform in plenty of time. He fired the shot during some loud passage, probably during the infernal row of the "Battle" section,* and I knew already that he had sent it into one of those bales containing strips of the old carpet, for when I went to examine the place for some clue to satisfy Higgy's craving for material facts, lo and behold! there was the hole of a shot in one of them, though it had evidently been carefully turned towards the wall for the purpose of avoiding or at least delaying detection. When I ripped

---

* No, dear Alan: the real noise of the "Battle" section does not begin until after the trumpeters are back in the orchestra. But there is a brief climax in the "Love" episode before the trumpet fanfare (pages 73–4 of the miniature score), followed almost immediately by rests for the violas taking up six and a half bars of moderately slow tempo and lasting, I should say, some 25 seconds.—J. H.

the bale open with my pocket-knife and unrolled the carpet, I found the hole neatly repeated at regular intervals nearly halfway through, until I came upon, not the brother, but the first cousin (same calibre, of course) of the bullet found in N. G.

During some pause in the viola parts, or perhaps only while Gough ceased playing for a moment, Holborne calmly handed the revolver through the hole just behind him, again on Lovelock's principle that these things infallibly succeed because they are never noticed, and are not noticed because they are not expected.* We must not forget that Gough, too, knew something about music-hall tricks and about the ease with which audiences can be assumed not to notice things. And so the revolver was ready, warm, and reeking, to be thrown in front of the unsuspecting but presently to be suspected Dashwood.

You may ask, as I did, why Holborne should not have shot N. G. from behind the hole during the row of the battle. There are two quite good explanations. According to Lovelock, who was however prejudiced in these matters, as you have seen, Holborne was no shot—and indeed why should a trumpeter be? According to Gough, I hear, he had firmly resisted the suggestion, actually made to him by his lodger, because suspicion would be much too likely to fall on him, as one of only three people hidden behind that partition, and he was not prepared to commit himself so far. Otherwise he ran hardly any risk at all. Both he and Gough knew that the main risk was Lovelock's, and he in turn cared comparatively little about being found out.

And so I come to the final and horribly tragic account. The

---

* Musicians, of course, can accurately time any proposed action to coincide with a passage in the music agreed upon beforehand.—J. H.

horror is softened only by my knowledge that I was able to do my best to let that poor dupe of circumstance off as lightly as possible. I repeat, if only to reassure myself, that I cannot feel I have done wrong, though we must of course keep quiet about this, as doctors have to do when they decide to give some incurable sufferer of agonies a little extra dose to help him along into another existence or into non-existence, both equally painless, whichever they happen to believe in. Fortunately, as Masterman had taken charge of Gough, I was able to deal with Lovelock in my own way; otherwise I should doubtless have been compelled to make a definite arrest at once. Well, I decided to risk it, the responsibility, though overwhelmingly great in a way, being in practice negligible; so don't go calling me a hero for risking my job or a criminal for imperilling your and the babes' existence. I felt sure of the Police, of the positive fortress which L.'s diggings happened to make under guard, and as a matter of fact of his playing the game. I doubt whether he would have tried to escape if he'd had a possible chance, for what was there for him to do or to look forward to? As a matter of fact he did escape—in his own way—but that's beyond human law. I'm glad he did, and he must have been dead at once. His weapons, of course, had been confiscated, but he found as good a way out.

He told me the story of his life during that quarter of an hour's walk to his room. An unrelieved tale of frustration, beginning with a father who beat him and a brother who was always getting preference, and ending with this sickening infatuation for Gwenny Jarvis, whose kindness even, little soft-hearted fool that she is, made things worse instead of better. But I won't sadden you by going into the harrowing details. I feel grisly enough myself. About the other two as well, in a lesser way. Of course they are only accessories before the fact, but that's bad enough.

My feelings are not improved by the necessity of staying on here and not seeing you and the kids just yet. I think perhaps I shall now go back to the Gillighans after all. I don't, like Beatrice, find Humphrey at all "intolerable," even as an affectation; in fact I see now how much I like him, judging by my immense relief at his not being a murderer. But perhaps that's mainly because I should not want the husband of a friend of yours to be anything of the sort; for I like you very much too. In fact... oh well, you know. And the dear kids. I must hie me once more to Pollock's in Saltergate for some more M'pool Lumps. I'd have brought them home in person, but alas...!

All my love till we meet,

and more thereafter,

ALAN.

P.S. I rang up Beatrice to ask if she could have me, and she is so elated—she little knows!—about what she actually dares to call the "satisfactory solution" (with sundry undeserved compliments for me) that she wants to celebrate it all in some way. Lord! But I confess that the manner of celebration she suggests means the seventh heaven for me, or the umpteenth, if seven isn't the limit. She wants you and the children to come here and we're all to stay at the G.s' (Letty included) and make it a nice house-party. I am not asking if you will come; I command you to pack up and leave by the first good train you can catch. Hurrah!

**If you've enjoyed *Death on the Down Beat*,
you won't want to miss**

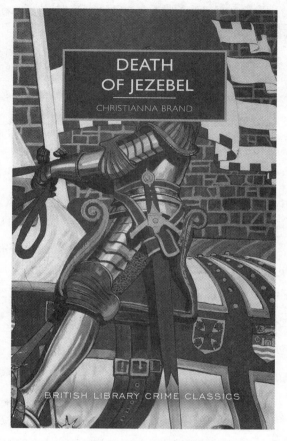

DEATH
OF JEZEBEL

CHRISTIANNA BRAND

BRITISH LIBRARY CRIME CLASSICS

the most recent BRITISH LIBRARY CRIME CLASSIC
published by Poisoned Pen Press, an imprint of Sourcebooks.

Praise for the
British Library Crime Classics

"Carr is at the top of his game in this taut whodunit... The British Library Crime Classics series has unearthed another worthy golden age puzzle."

—*Publishers Weekly*, STARRED Review,
for *The Lost Gallows*

"A wonderful rediscovery."
—*Booklist*, STARRED Review, for *The Sussex Downs Murder*

"First-rate mystery and an engrossing view into a vanished world."
—*Booklist*, STARRED Review, for *Death of an Airman*

"A cunningly concocted locked-room mystery, a staple of Golden Age detective fiction."
—*Booklist*, STARRED Review, for *Murder of a Lady*

"The book is both utterly of its time and utterly ahead of it."
—*New York Times Book Review* for *The Notting Hill Mystery*

"As with the best of such compilations, readers of classic mysteries will relish discovering unfamiliar authors, along with old favorites such as Arthur Conan Doyle and G.K. Chesterton."
—*Publishers Weekly*, STARRED Review, for *Continental Crimes*

"In this imaginative anthology, Edwards—president of Britain's Detection Club—has gathered together overlooked criminous gems."
—*Washington Post* for *Crimson Snow*

"The degree of suspense Crofts achieves by showing the growing obsession and planning is worthy of Hitchcock. Another first-rate reissue from the British Library Crime Classics series."
—*Booklist*, STARRED Review, for *The 12.30 from Croydon*

"Not only is this a first-rate puzzler, but Crofts's outrage over the financial firm's betrayal of the public trust should resonate with today's readers."
—*Booklist*, STARRED Review, for *Mystery in the Channel*

"This reissue exemplifies the mission of the British Library Crime Classics series in making an outstanding and original mystery accessible to a modern audience."
—*Publishers Weekly*, STARRED Review, for *Excellent Intentions*

"A book to delight every puzzle-suspense enthusiast"
—*New York Times* for *The Colour of Murder*

"Edwards's outstanding third winter-themed anthology showcases 11 uniformly clever and entertaining stories, mostly from lesser known authors, providing further evidence of the editor's expertise...This entry in the British Library Crime Classics series will be a welcome holiday gift for fans of the golden age of detection."
—*Publishers Weekly*, STARRED Review, for *The Christmas Card Crime and Other Stories*

poisonedpenpress.com